W9-CFG-107

SUMMER CAMP
SCIENCE
MYSTERIES

#4 The Werewolf Chase

A Mystery
about Adaptations

by Lynda Beauregard
illustrated by German Torres

GRAPHIC UNIVERSE™ • MINNEAPOLIS • NEW YORK

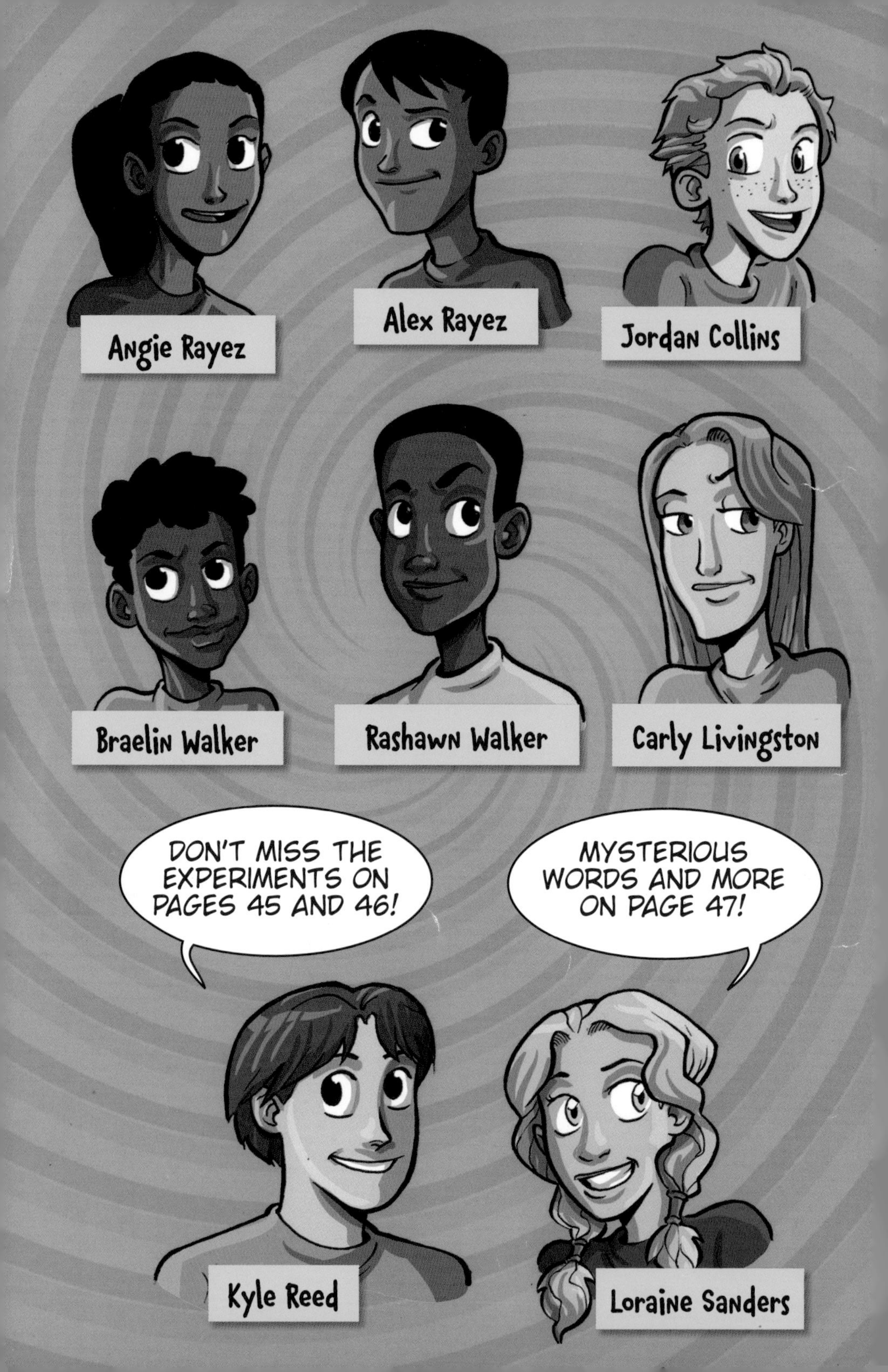
Angie Rayez
Alex Rayez
Jordan Collins
Braelin Walker
Rashawn Walker
Carly Livingston
DON'T MISS THE EXPERIMENTS ON PAGES 45 AND 46!
MYSTERIOUS WORDS AND MORE ON PAGE 47!
Kyle Reed
Loraine Sanders

Plants and animals adapt, or make themselves suited, to the conditions of the environment in which they live. Specialized body parts help animals obtain food, stay warm or cool, evade predators, and reproduce. Beaks, long ears, claws, fingers, and fur color are examples of physical adaptations. Behavioral adaptations include migration (moving from one area to another), hibernation (resting during winter), and playing dead to fool a predator.

Story by Lynda Beauregard
Art by German Torres
Coloring by Jenn Manley Lee
Lettering by Grace Lu

Copyright © 2012 by Lerner Publishing Group, Inc.

Graphic Universe™ is a trademark of Lerner Publishing Group, Inc.

Graphic Universe™
A division of Lerner Publishing Group, Inc.
241 First Avenue North
Minneapolis, MN 55401 U.S.A.

Website address: www.lernerbooks.com

Main body text set in CCWildwords.
Typeface provided by Comicraft/Active Images.

Library of Congress Cataloging-in-Publication Data

Beauregard, Lynda.
    The werewolf chase : a mystery about adaptations / by Lynda Beauregard ;
    illustrated by German Torres.
        p.   cm. — (Summer camp science mysteries)
        Summary: While studying animal adaptations and then noticing a camp
    counselor's suspicious late-night activities, campers begin to fear that the counselor
    is really a werewolf. Includes glossary and experiments.
        ISBN: 978–0–7613–5691–2 (lib. bdg. : alk. paper)
        1. Graphic novels. [1. Graphic novels. 2. Camps—Fiction. 3. Animals—
    Adaptation—Fiction.] I. Torres, German, ill. II. Title.
    PZ7.7.B42We 2012
    741.5'973—dc23   2011016583

Manufactured in the United States of America
1 – CG – 12/31/11

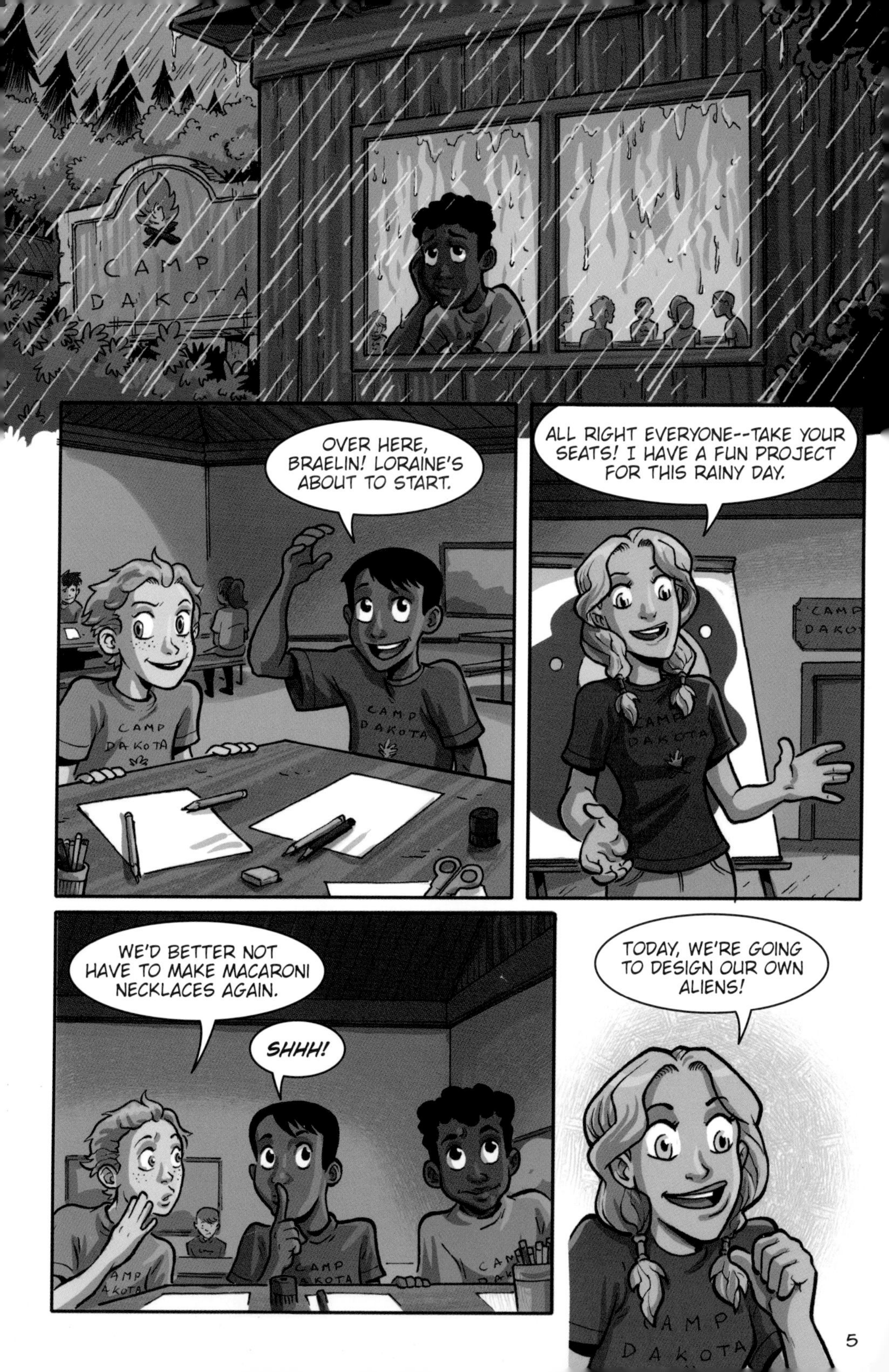
CAMP DAKOTA
OVER HERE, BRAELIN! LORAINE'S ABOUT TO START.
ALL RIGHT EVERYONE--TAKE YOUR SEATS! I HAVE A FUN PROJECT FOR THIS RAINY DAY.
WE'D BETTER NOT HAVE TO MAKE MACARONI NECKLACES AGAIN.
SHHH!
TODAY, WE'RE GOING TO DESIGN OUR OWN ALIENS!

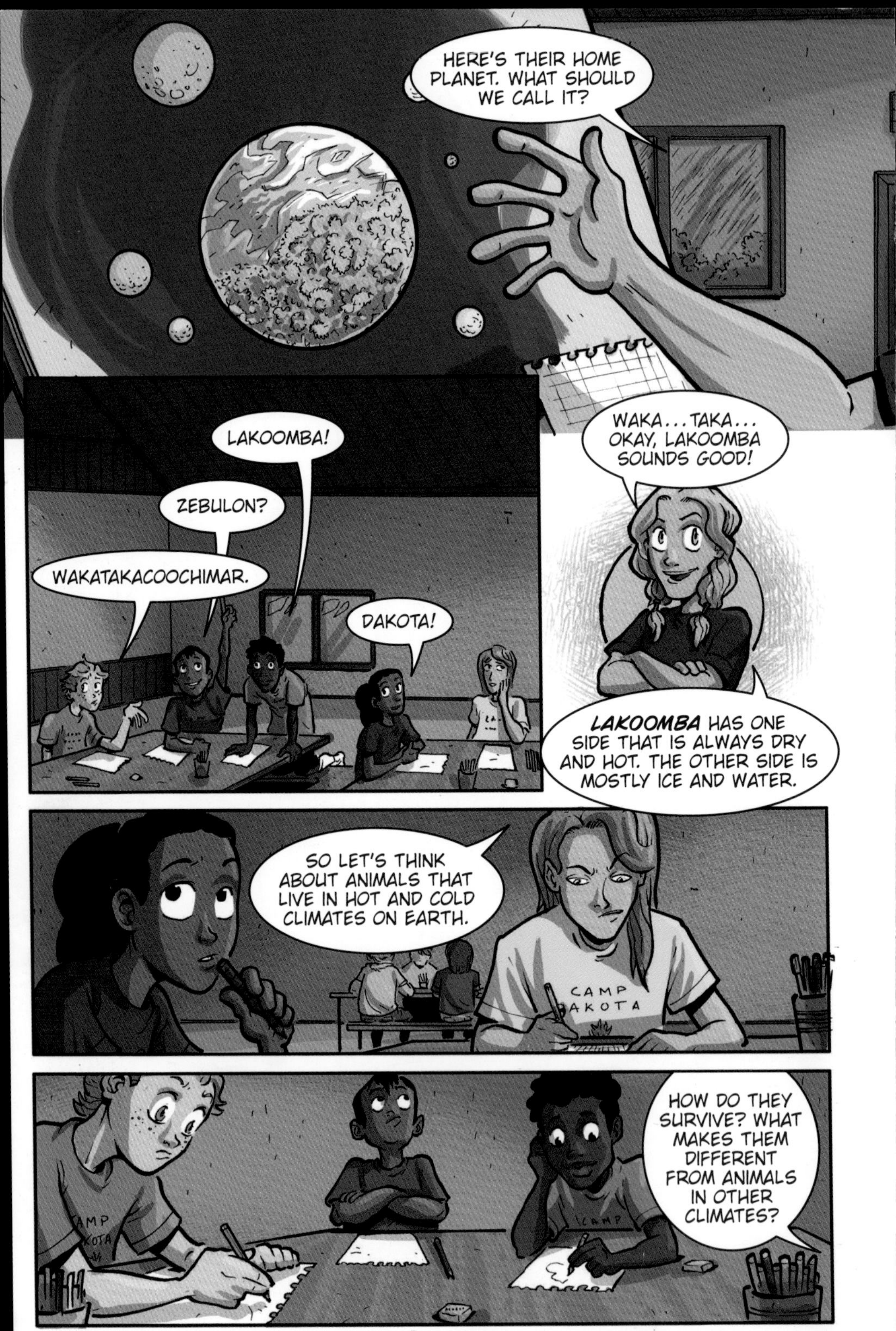
HERE'S THEIR HOME PLANET. WHAT SHOULD WE CALL IT?
WAKATAKACOOCHIMAR.
ZEBULON?
LAKOOMBA!
DAKOTA!
WAKA . . . TAKA . . . OKAY, LAKOOMBA SOUNDS GOOD!
LAKOOMBA HAS ONE SIDE THAT IS ALWAYS DRY AND HOT. THE OTHER SIDE IS MOSTLY ICE AND WATER.
SO LET'S THINK ABOUT ANIMALS THAT LIVE IN HOT AND COLD CLIMATES ON EARTH.
CAMP DAKOTA
HOW DO THEY SURVIVE? WHAT MAKES THEM DIFFERENT FROM ANIMALS IN OTHER CLIMATES?

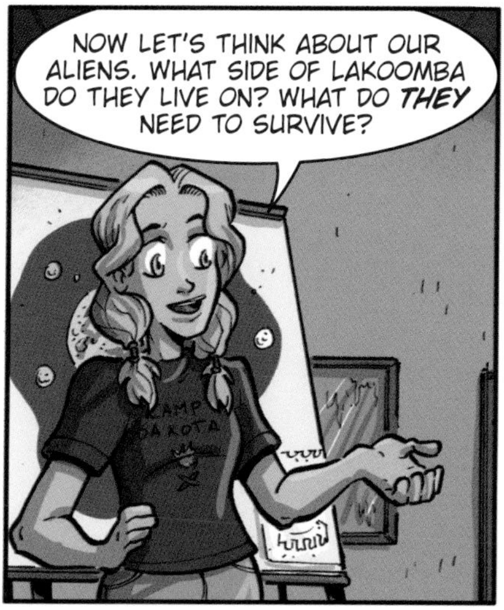
NOW LET'S THINK ABOUT OUR ALIENS. WHAT SIDE OF LAKOOMBA DO THEY LIVE ON? WHAT DO *THEY* NEED TO SURVIVE?

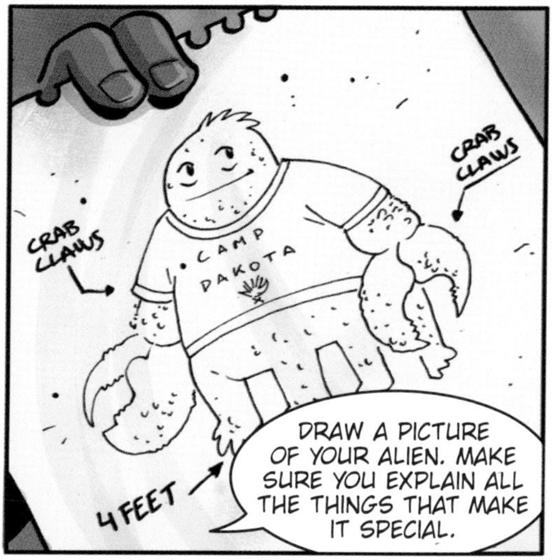
CRAB CLAWS
CAMP DAKOTA
CRAB CLAWS
4 FEET
DRAW A PICTURE OF YOUR ALIEN. MAKE SURE YOU EXPLAIN ALL THE THINGS THAT MAKE IT SPECIAL.

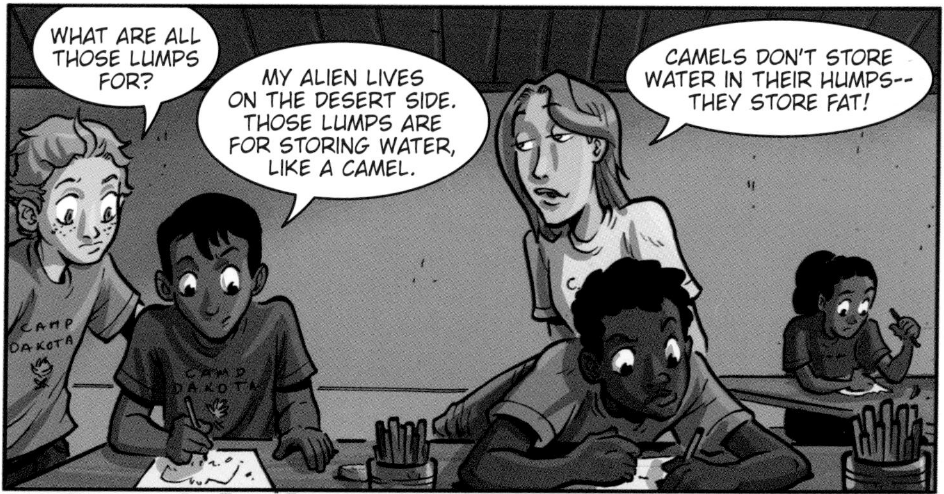
WHAT ARE ALL THOSE LUMPS FOR?
MY ALIEN LIVES ON THE DESERT SIDE. THOSE LUMPS ARE FOR STORING WATER, LIKE A CAMEL.
CAMELS DON'T STORE WATER IN THEIR HUMPS--THEY STORE FAT!

Camels use stored fat as a source of energy. When a camel's body turns fat into energy, the process also releases water into the camel's system.

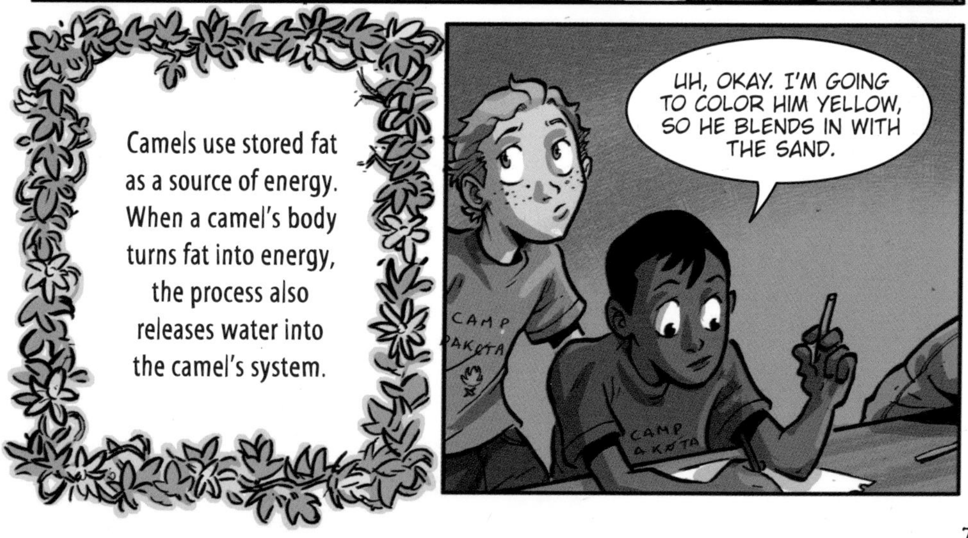
UH, OKAY. I'M GOING TO COLOR HIM YELLOW, SO HE BLENDS IN WITH THE SAND.

MY ALIEN CAN FLY, SO HE STAYS IN THE DESERT AT NIGHT AND HEADS FOR THE COOLER SIDE DURING THE DAY.
CAMP DAKOTA
WHY DOESN'T HE HAVE A BEAK?
HE DOESN'T NEED ONE--HE'S GOT HANDS.
ANGIE'S ALIEN DOESN'T HAVE A NOSE OR EARS.
YES, SHE DOES. THEY'RE JUST SMALL.
SHE'S LIKE A RIVER OTTER. SHE CLOSES HER NOSE AND EARS WHEN SHE GOES UNDERWATER.
AND SHE HAS TWO LAYERS OF FUR TO KEEP HER WARM AND WATERPROOF.

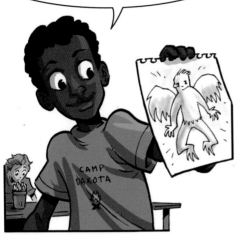

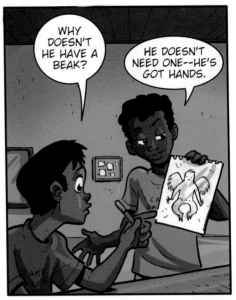

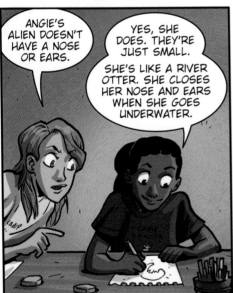

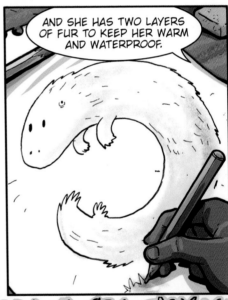

River otters are mammals, but they're well suited to water travel. These creatures can slow their pulse to one-tenth its normal rate to conserve oxygen when they dive.

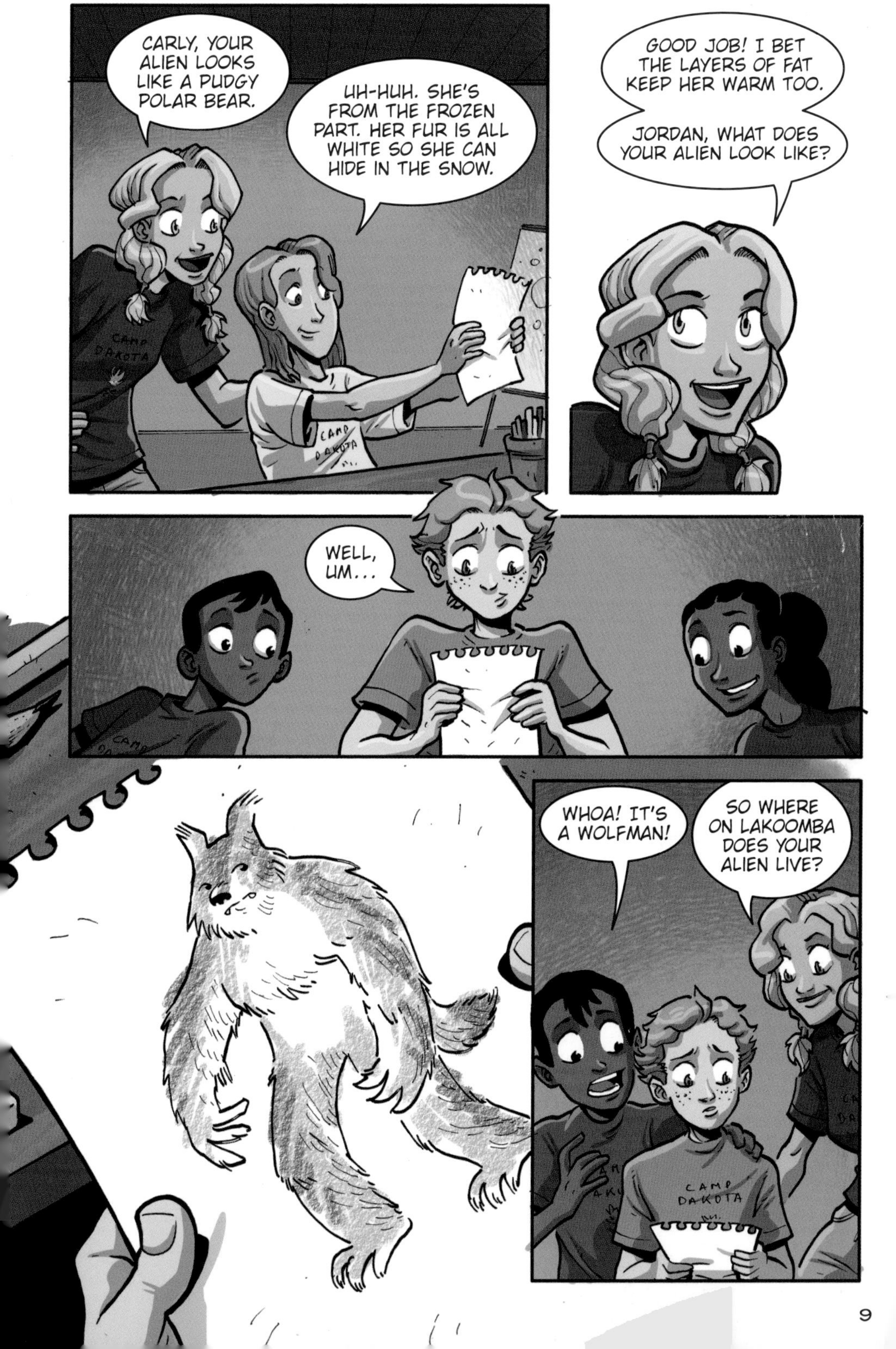
CARLY, YOUR ALIEN LOOKS LIKE A PUDGY POLAR BEAR.
UH-HUH. SHE'S FROM THE FROZEN PART. HER FUR IS ALL WHITE SO SHE CAN HIDE IN THE SNOW.
GOOD JOB! I BET THE LAYERS OF FAT KEEP HER WARM TOO.
JORDAN, WHAT DOES YOUR ALIEN LOOK LIKE?
CAMP DAKOTA
WELL, UM...
WHOA! IT'S A WOLFMAN!
SO WHERE ON LAKOOMBA DOES YOUR ALIEN LIVE?
CAMP DAKOTA

BOTH SIDES, I GUESS.

GRAY WOLVES HAVE WOOLY FUR AND THICK FOOT PADS FOR WARMTH.

AND THEIR CLAWS CAN SPREAD WIDE FOR BETTER FOOTING IN THE SNOW.

BUT ARABIAN WOLVES CAN SURVIVE IN THE DESERT.

THEIR FUR GETS SHORT IN THE SUMMER, AND THEIR LONG EARS HELP THEM STAY COOL.

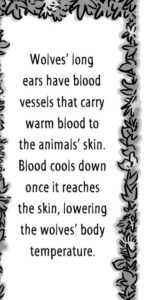

Wolves' long ears have blood vessels that carry warm blood to the animals' skin. Blood cools down once it reaches the skin, lowering the wolves' body temperature.

WOW. YOU SURE KNOW A LOT ABOUT WOLVES.

I'VE READ A BUNCH OF BOOKS.

YAY! LET'S HEAD BACK TO THE MAIN CABIN--

--AND GET SOME DINNER.

I'M HUNGRY!

NICE WORK ALL AROUND!

AND LOOK--WHILE YOU WERE WORKING ON YOUR ALIENS, THE RAIN STOPPED.

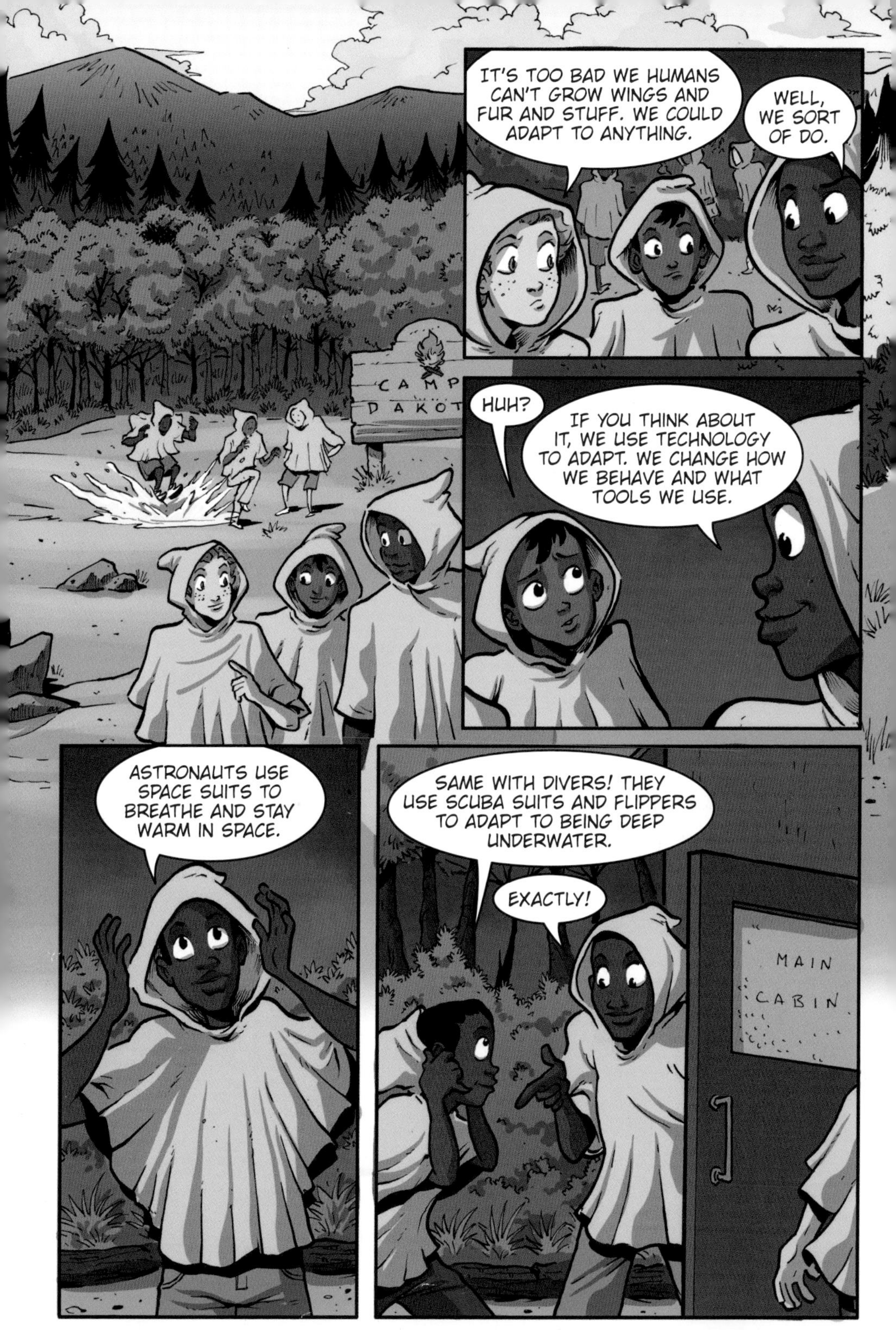
CAMP
DAKOT
IT'S TOO BAD WE HUMANS CAN'T GROW WINGS AND FUR AND STUFF. WE COULD ADAPT TO ANYTHING.
WELL, WE SORT OF DO.
HUH?
IF YOU THINK ABOUT IT, WE USE TECHNOLOGY TO ADAPT. WE CHANGE HOW WE BEHAVE AND WHAT TOOLS WE USE.
ASTRONAUTS USE SPACE SUITS TO BREATHE AND STAY WARM IN SPACE.
SAME WITH DIVERS! THEY USE SCUBA SUITS AND FLIPPERS TO ADAPT TO BEING DEEP UNDERWATER.
EXACTLY!
MAIN CABIN

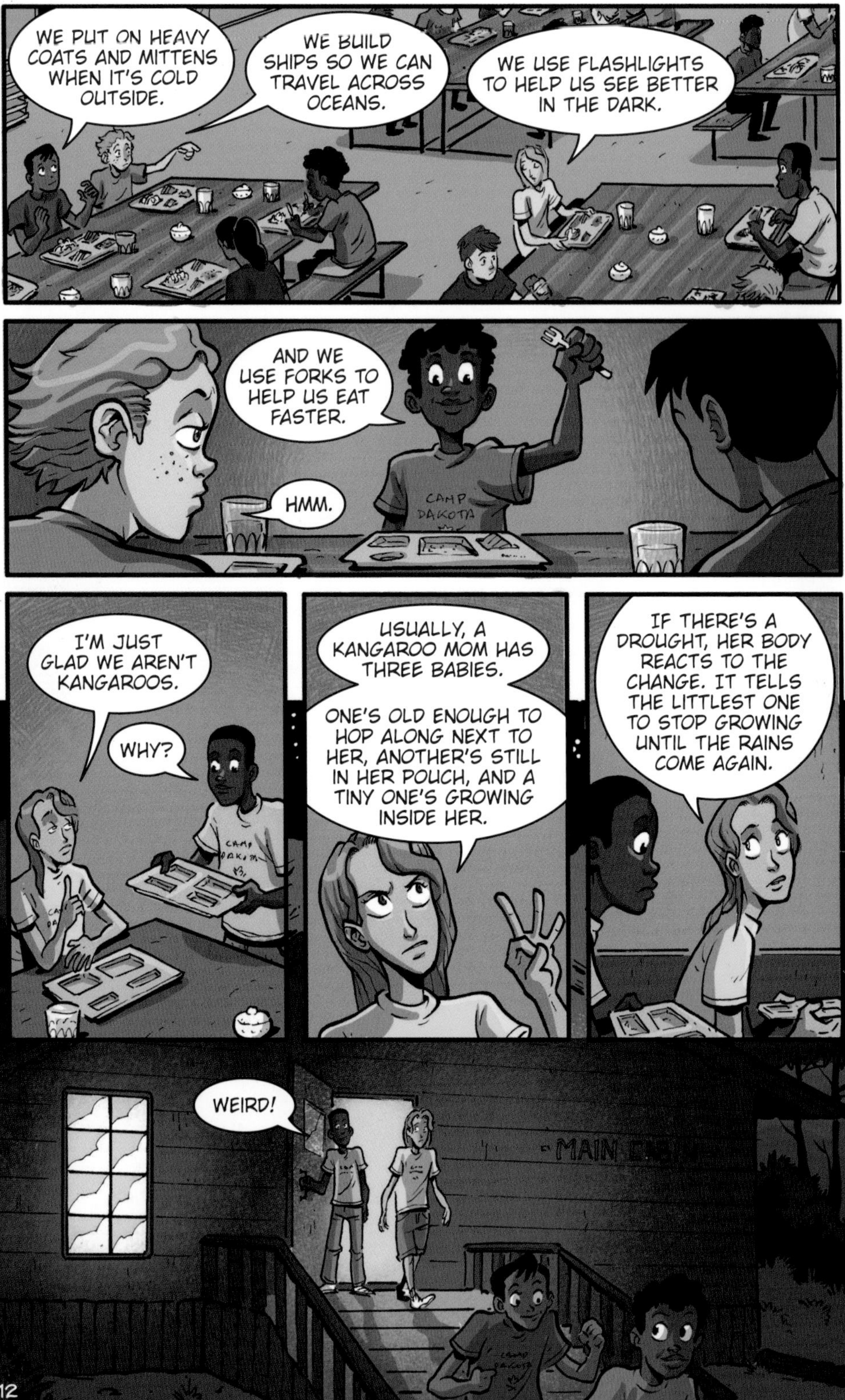
WE PUT ON HEAVY COATS AND MITTENS WHEN IT'S COLD OUTSIDE.
WE BUILD SHIPS SO WE CAN TRAVEL ACROSS OCEANS.
WE USE FLASHLIGHTS TO HELP US SEE BETTER IN THE DARK.
AND WE USE FORKS TO HELP US EAT FASTER.
HMM.
CAMP DAKOTA
I'M JUST GLAD WE AREN'T KANGAROOS.
WHY?
USUALLY, A KANGAROO MOM HAS THREE BABIES.
ONE'S OLD ENOUGH TO HOP ALONG NEXT TO HER, ANOTHER'S STILL IN HER POUCH, AND A TINY ONE'S GROWING INSIDE HER.
IF THERE'S A DROUGHT, HER BODY REACTS TO THE CHANGE. IT TELLS THE LITTLEST ONE TO STOP GROWING UNTIL THE RAINS COME AGAIN.
WEIRD!

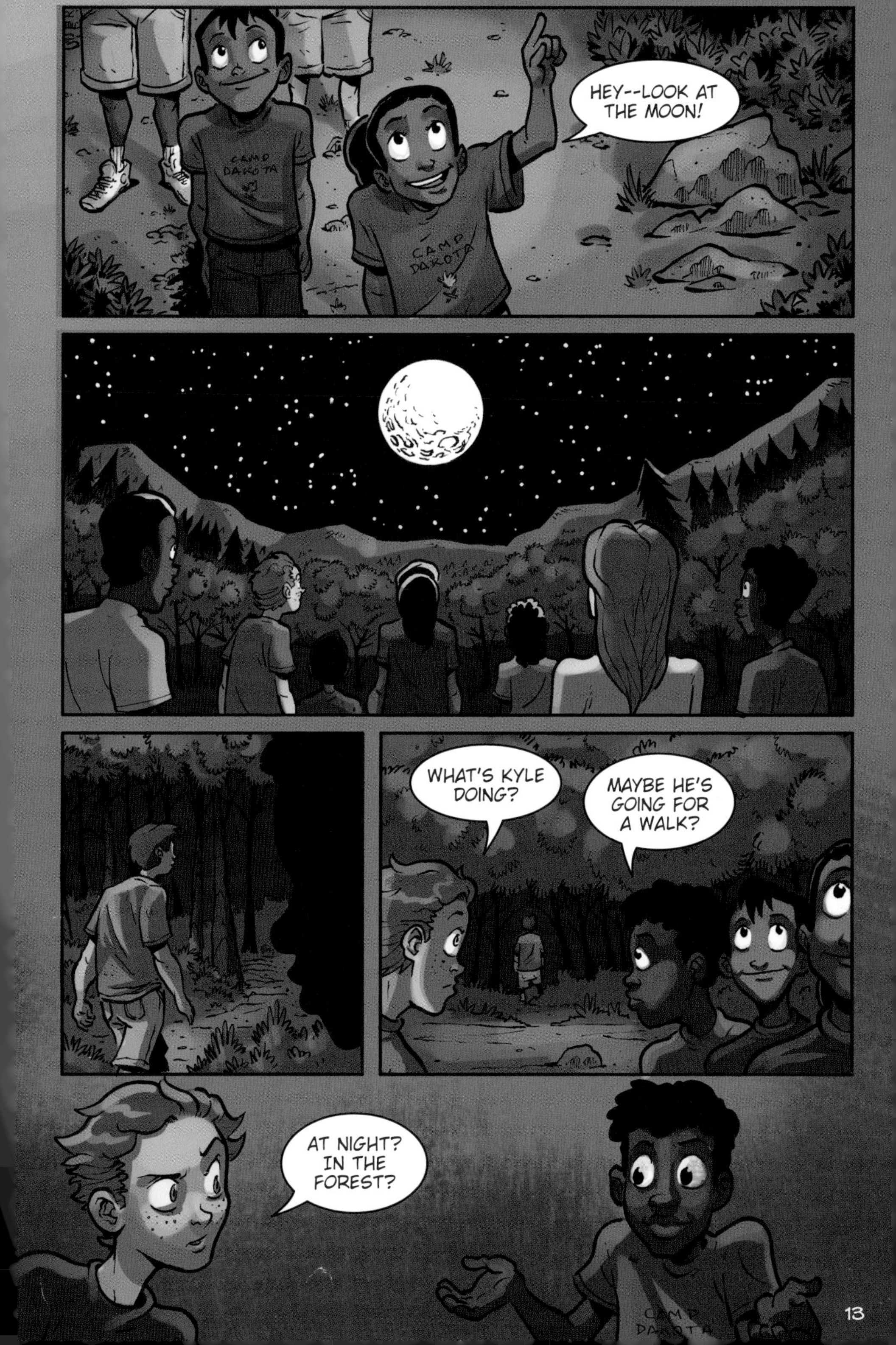

HEY--LOOK AT THE MOON!
CAMP DAKOTA
CAMP DAKOTA
WHAT'S KYLE DOING?
MAYBE HE'S GOING FOR A WALK?
AT NIGHT? IN THE FOREST?

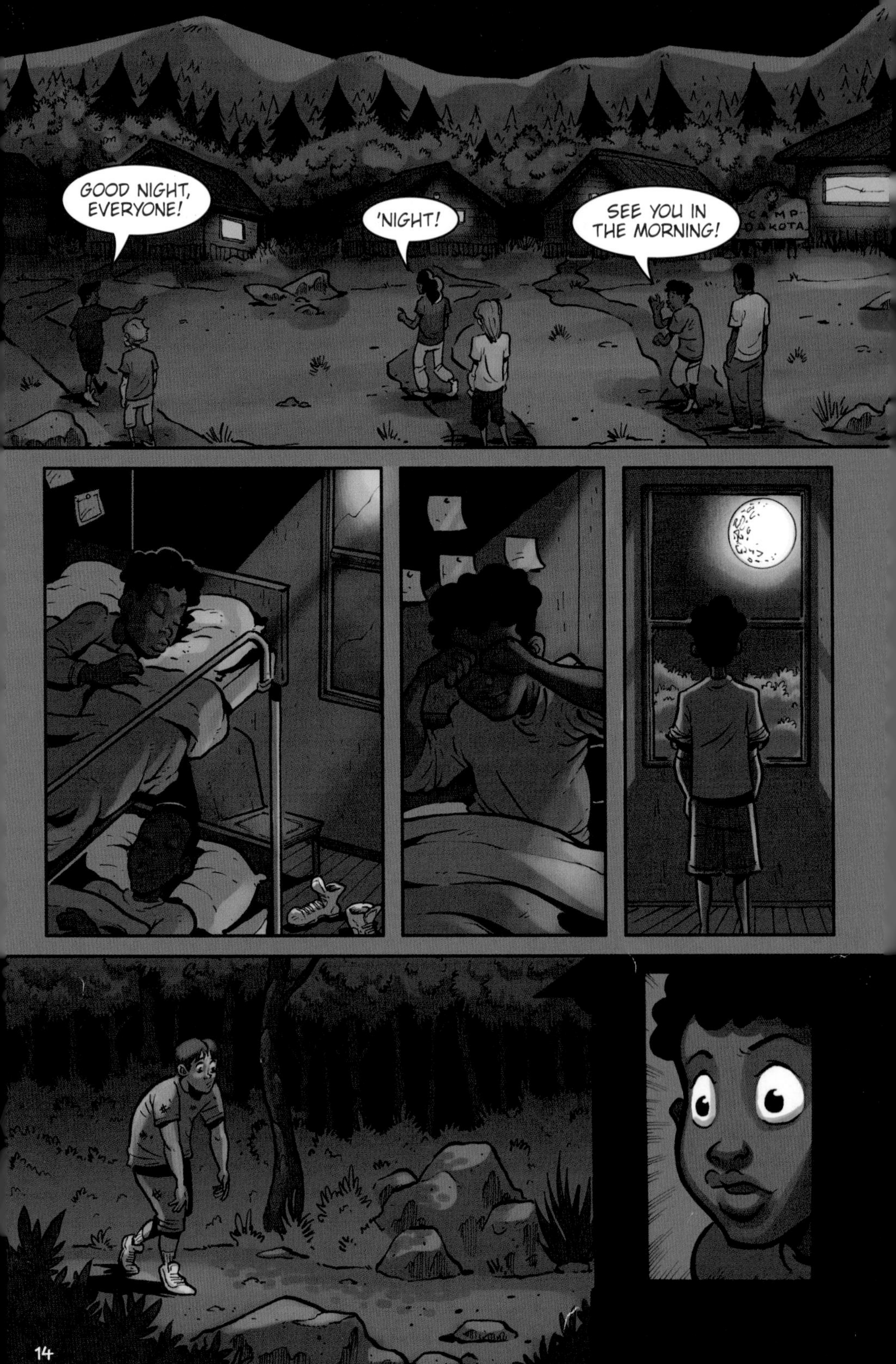
GOOD NIGHT, EVERYONE!
'NIGHT!
SEE YOU IN THE MORNING!
CAMP DAKOTA

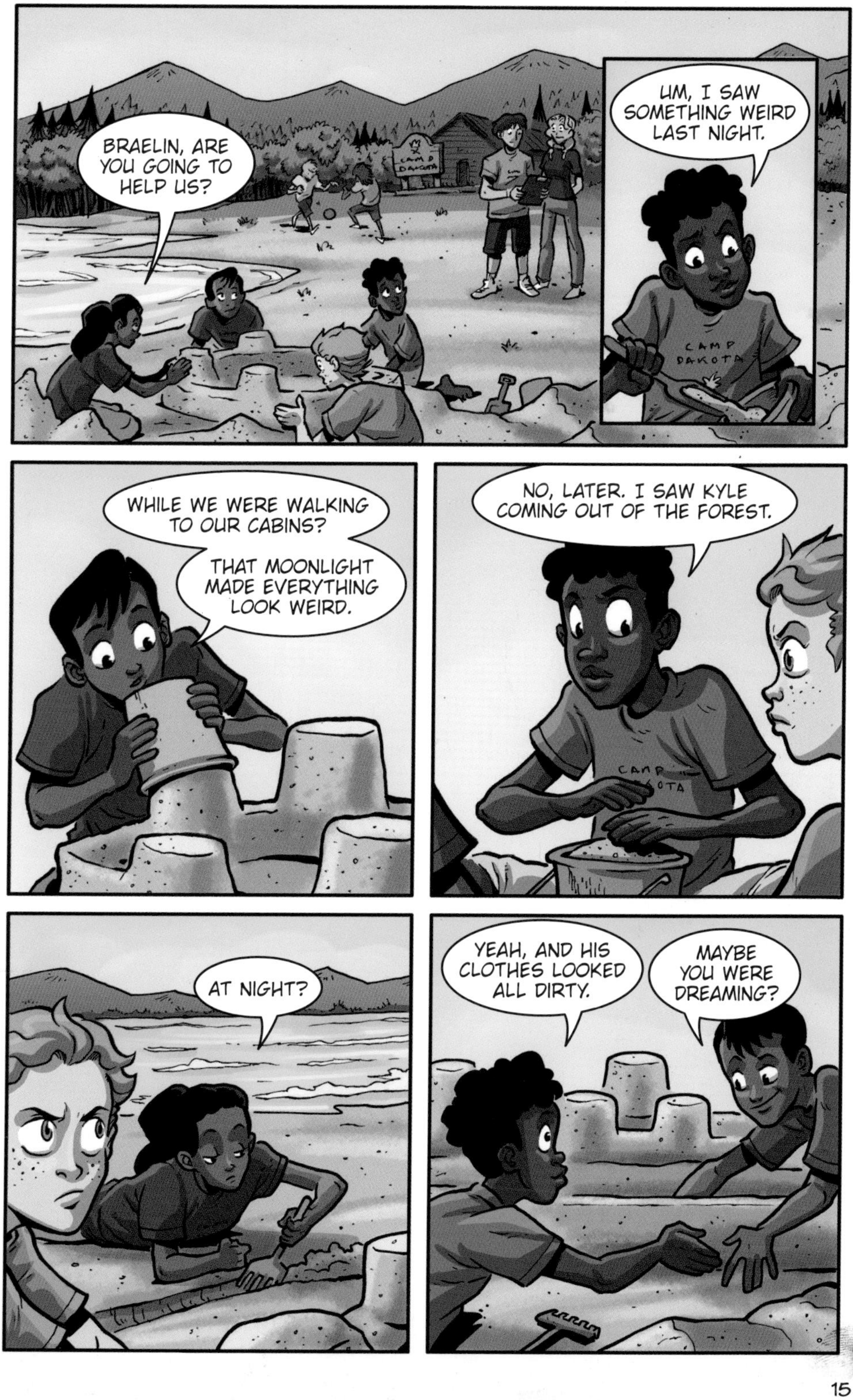
BRAELIN, ARE YOU GOING TO HELP US?
UM, I SAW SOMETHING WEIRD LAST NIGHT.
CAMP DAKOTA
WHILE WE WERE WALKING TO OUR CABINS?
THAT MOONLIGHT MADE EVERYTHING LOOK WEIRD.
NO, LATER. I SAW KYLE COMING OUT OF THE FOREST.
AT NIGHT?
YEAH, AND HIS CLOTHES LOOKED ALL DIRTY.
MAYBE YOU WERE DREAMING?

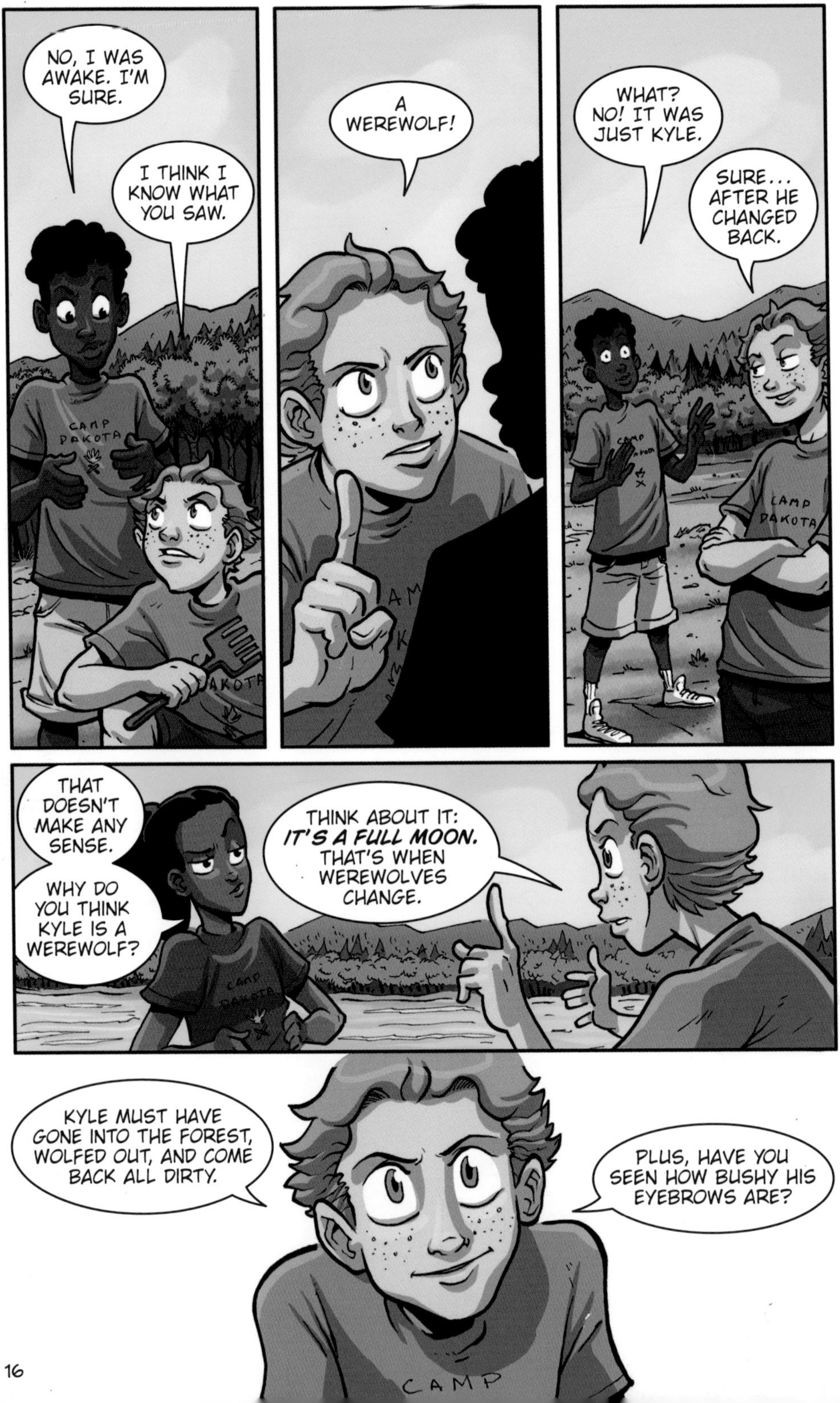
NO, I WAS AWAKE. I'M SURE.
I THINK I KNOW WHAT YOU SAW.
A WEREWOLF!
WHAT? NO! IT WAS JUST KYLE.
SURE... AFTER HE CHANGED BACK.
CAMP DAKOTA
THAT DOESN'T MAKE ANY SENSE.
WHY DO YOU THINK KYLE IS A WEREWOLF?
THINK ABOUT IT: *IT'S A FULL MOON.* THAT'S WHEN WEREWOLVES CHANGE.
KYLE MUST HAVE GONE INTO THE FOREST, WOLFED OUT, AND COME BACK ALL DIRTY.
PLUS, HAVE YOU SEEN HOW BUSHY HIS EYEBROWS ARE?
CAMP

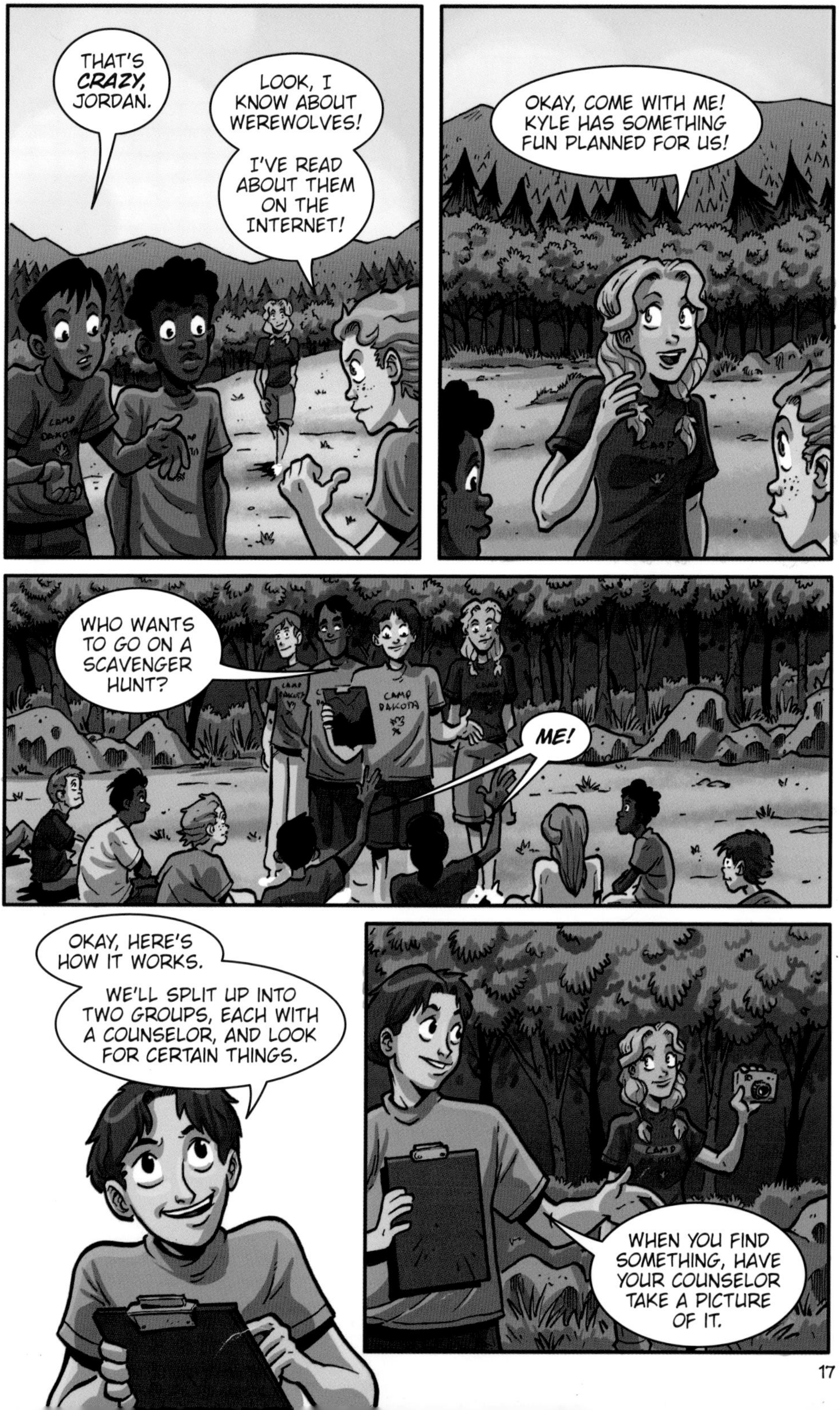
THAT'S **CRAZY,** JORDAN.
LOOK, I KNOW ABOUT WEREWOLVES!
I'VE READ ABOUT THEM ON THE INTERNET!
OKAY, COME WITH ME! KYLE HAS SOMETHING FUN PLANNED FOR US!
CAMP DAKOTA
WHO WANTS TO GO ON A SCAVENGER HUNT?
CAMP DAKOTA
ME!
OKAY, HERE'S HOW IT WORKS.
WE'LL SPLIT UP INTO TWO GROUPS, EACH WITH A COUNSELOR, AND LOOK FOR CERTAIN THINGS.
WHEN YOU FIND SOMETHING, HAVE YOUR COUNSELOR TAKE A PICTURE OF IT.

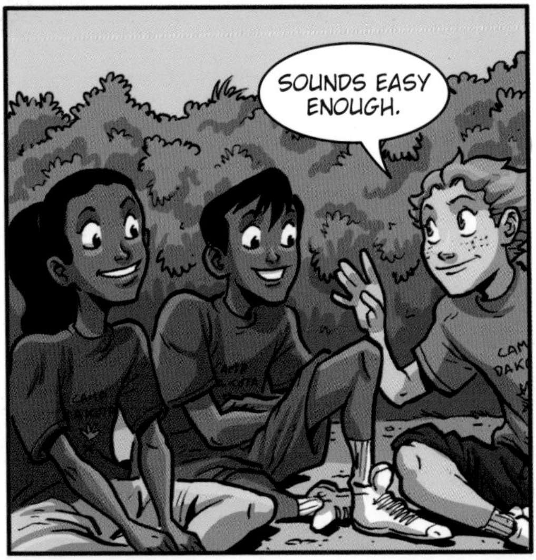
SOUNDS EASY ENOUGH.

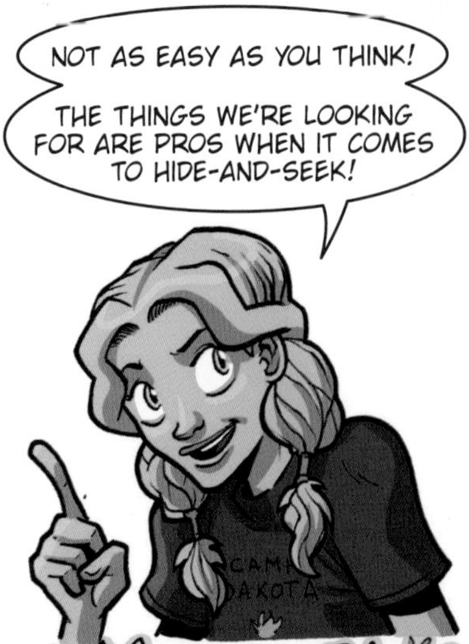
NOT AS EASY AS YOU THINK!
THE THINGS WE'RE LOOKING FOR ARE PROS WHEN IT COMES TO HIDE-AND-SEEK!

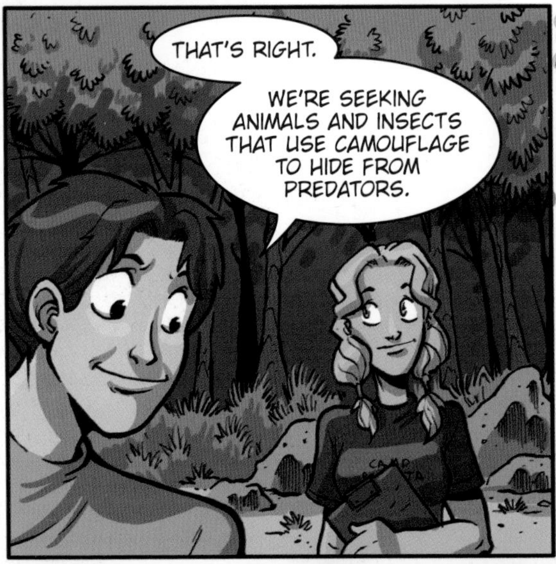
THAT'S RIGHT.
WE'RE SEEKING ANIMALS AND INSECTS THAT USE CAMOUFLAGE TO HIDE FROM PREDATORS.

Camouflage is a physical adaptation. Many animals and insects have colors or patterns on their skin or fur that allow them to blend in with their surroundings.

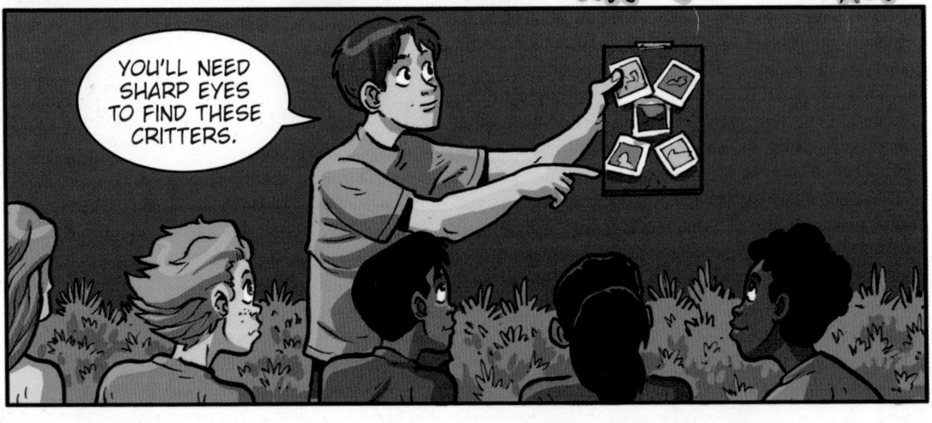
YOU'LL NEED SHARP EYES TO FIND THESE CRITTERS.

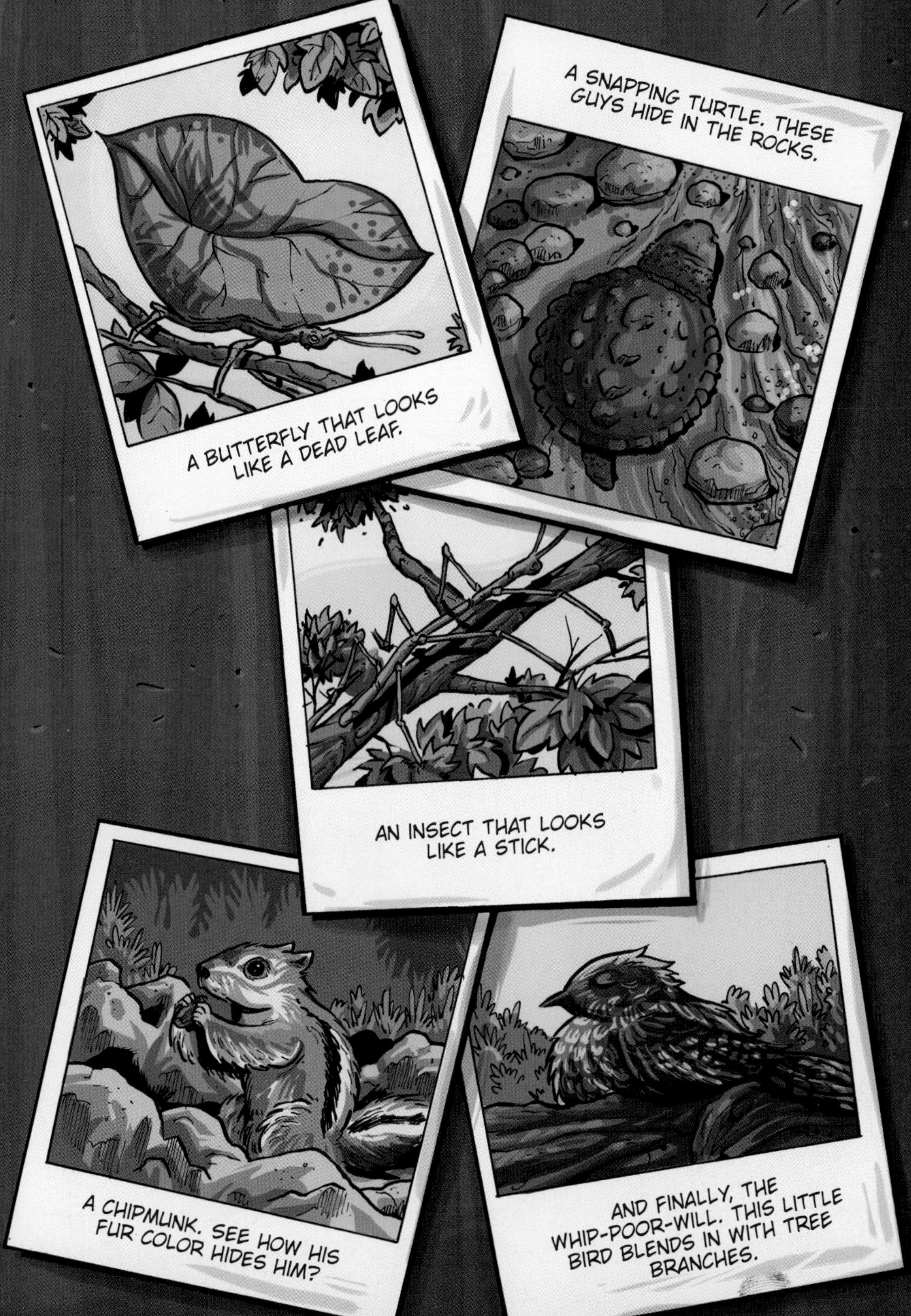
A BUTTERFLY THAT LOOKS LIKE A DEAD LEAF.
A SNAPPING TURTLE. THESE GUYS HIDE IN THE ROCKS.
AN INSECT THAT LOOKS LIKE A STICK.
A CHIPMUNK. SEE HOW HIS FUR COLOR HIDES HIM?
AND FINALLY, THE WHIP-POOR-WILL. THIS LITTLE BIRD BLENDS IN WITH TREE BRANCHES.

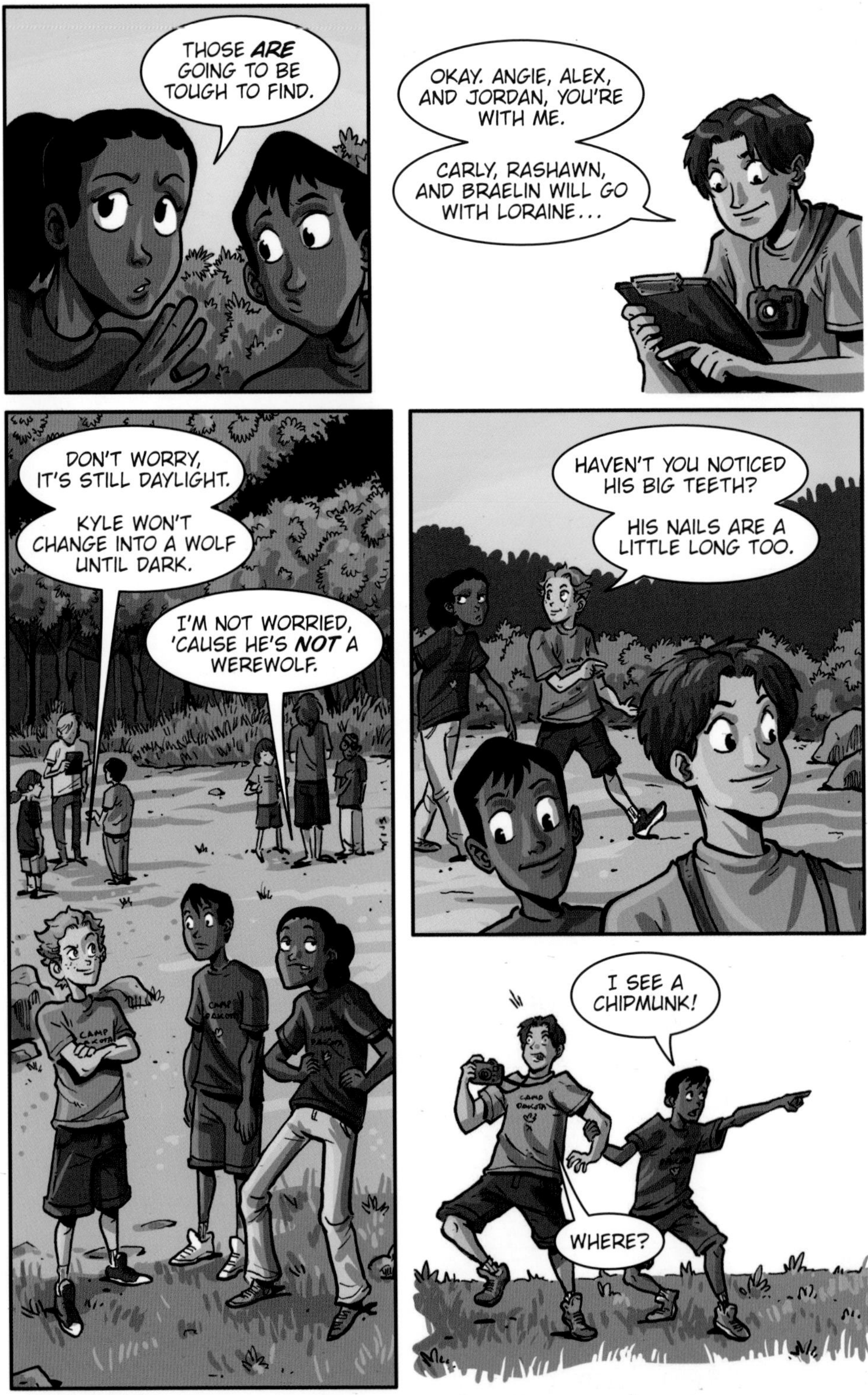
THOSE ARE GOING TO BE TOUGH TO FIND.
OKAY. ANGIE, ALEX, AND JORDAN, YOU'RE WITH ME.
CARLY, RASHAWN, AND BRAELIN WILL GO WITH LORAINE...
DON'T WORRY, IT'S STILL DAYLIGHT.
KYLE WON'T CHANGE INTO A WOLF UNTIL DARK.
I'M NOT WORRIED, 'CAUSE HE'S NOT A WEREWOLF.
HAVEN'T YOU NOTICED HIS BIG TEETH?
HIS NAILS ARE A LITTLE LONG TOO.
I SEE A CHIPMUNK!
WHERE?

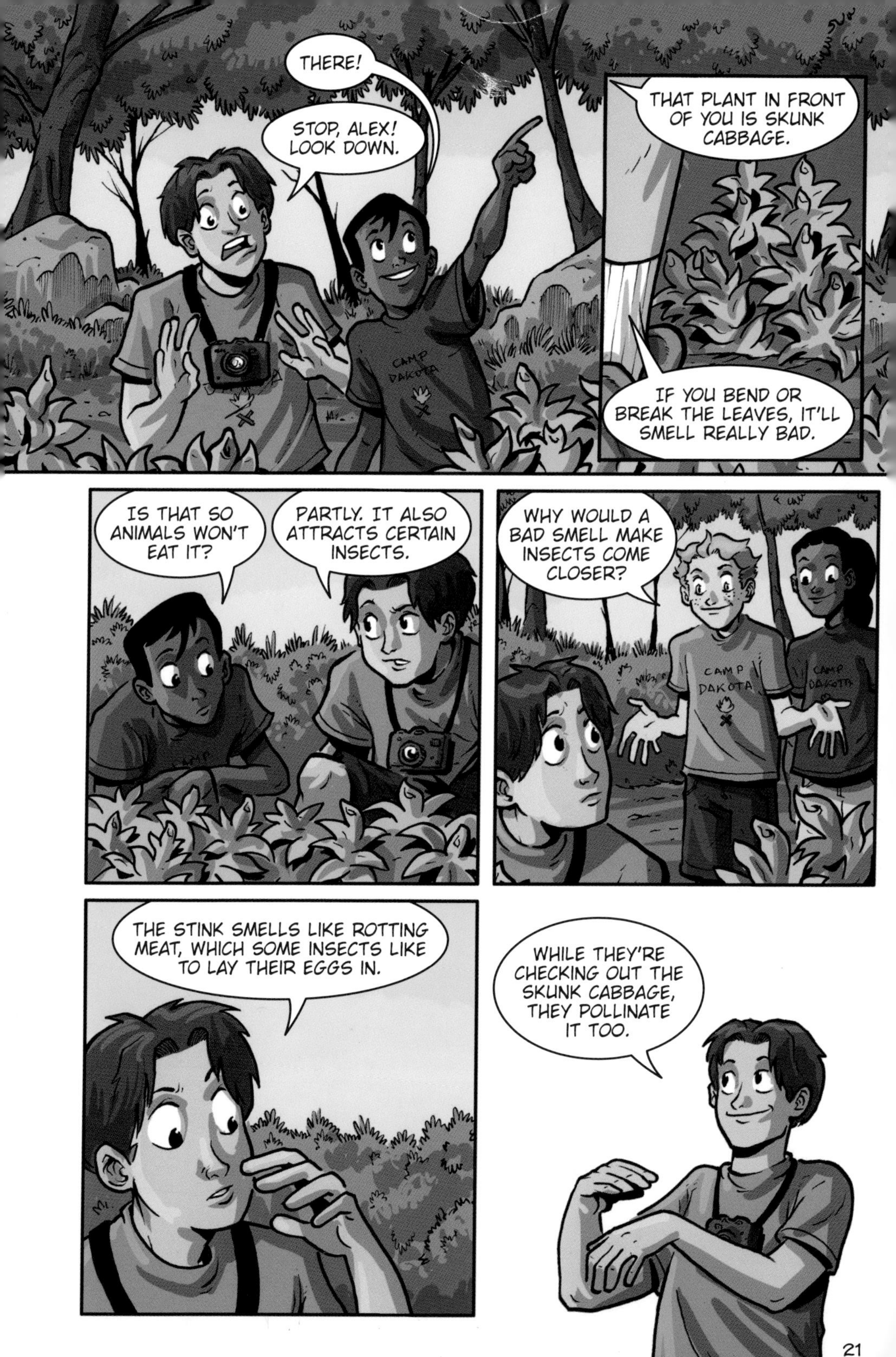

STOP, ALEX! LOOK DOWN.
THERE!
THAT PLANT IN FRONT OF YOU IS SKUNK CABBAGE.
IF YOU BEND OR BREAK THE LEAVES, IT'LL SMELL REALLY BAD.
CAMP DAKOTA
IS THAT SO ANIMALS WON'T EAT IT?
PARTLY. IT ALSO ATTRACTS CERTAIN INSECTS.
WHY WOULD A BAD SMELL MAKE INSECTS COME CLOSER?
CAMP DAKOTA
THE STINK SMELLS LIKE ROTTING MEAT, WHICH SOME INSECTS LIKE TO LAY THEIR EGGS IN.
WHILE THEY'RE CHECKING OUT THE SKUNK CABBAGE, THEY POLLINATE IT TOO.

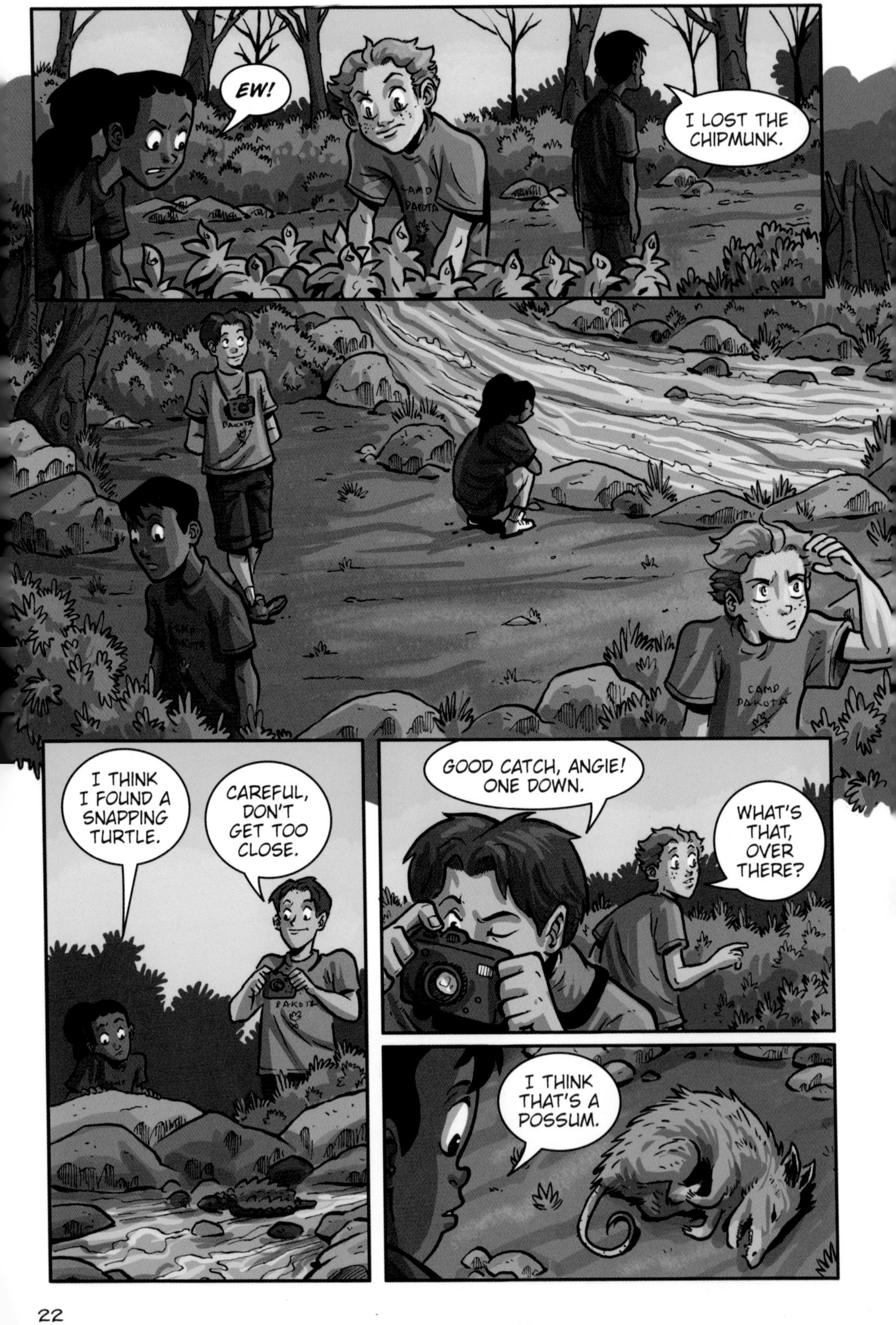
EW!
I LOST THE CHIPMUNK.
CAMP DAKOTA
I THINK I FOUND A SNAPPING TURTLE.
CAREFUL, DON'T GET TOO CLOSE.
GOOD CATCH, ANGIE! ONE DOWN.
WHAT'S THAT, OVER THERE?
I THINK THAT'S A POSSUM.

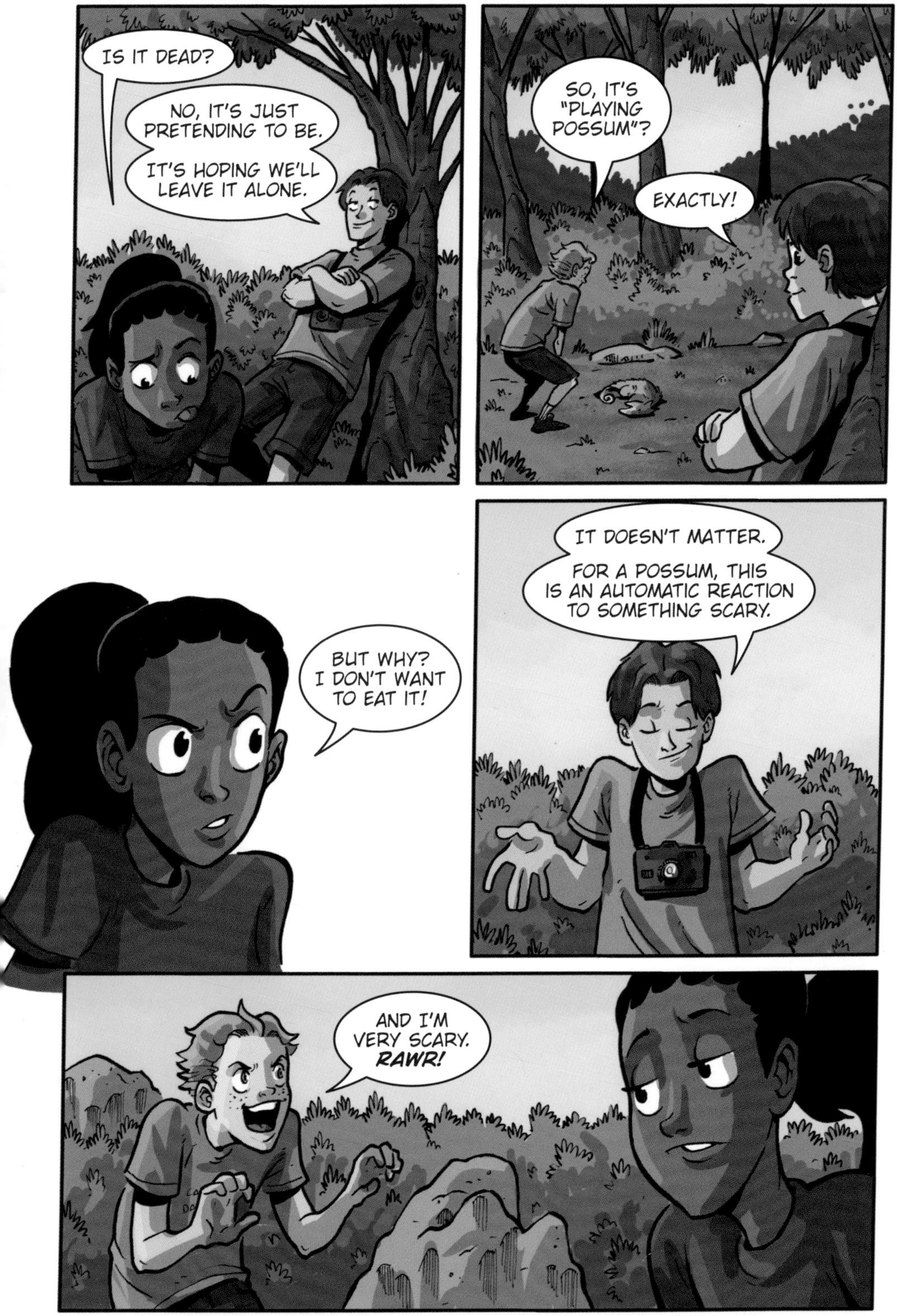
IS IT DEAD?
NO, IT'S JUST PRETENDING TO BE.
IT'S HOPING WE'LL LEAVE IT ALONE.
SO, IT'S "PLAYING POSSUM"?
EXACTLY!
BUT WHY? I DON'T WANT TO EAT IT!
IT DOESN'T MATTER.
FOR A POSSUM, THIS IS AN AUTOMATIC REACTION TO SOMETHING SCARY.
AND I'M VERY SCARY. ***RAWR!***

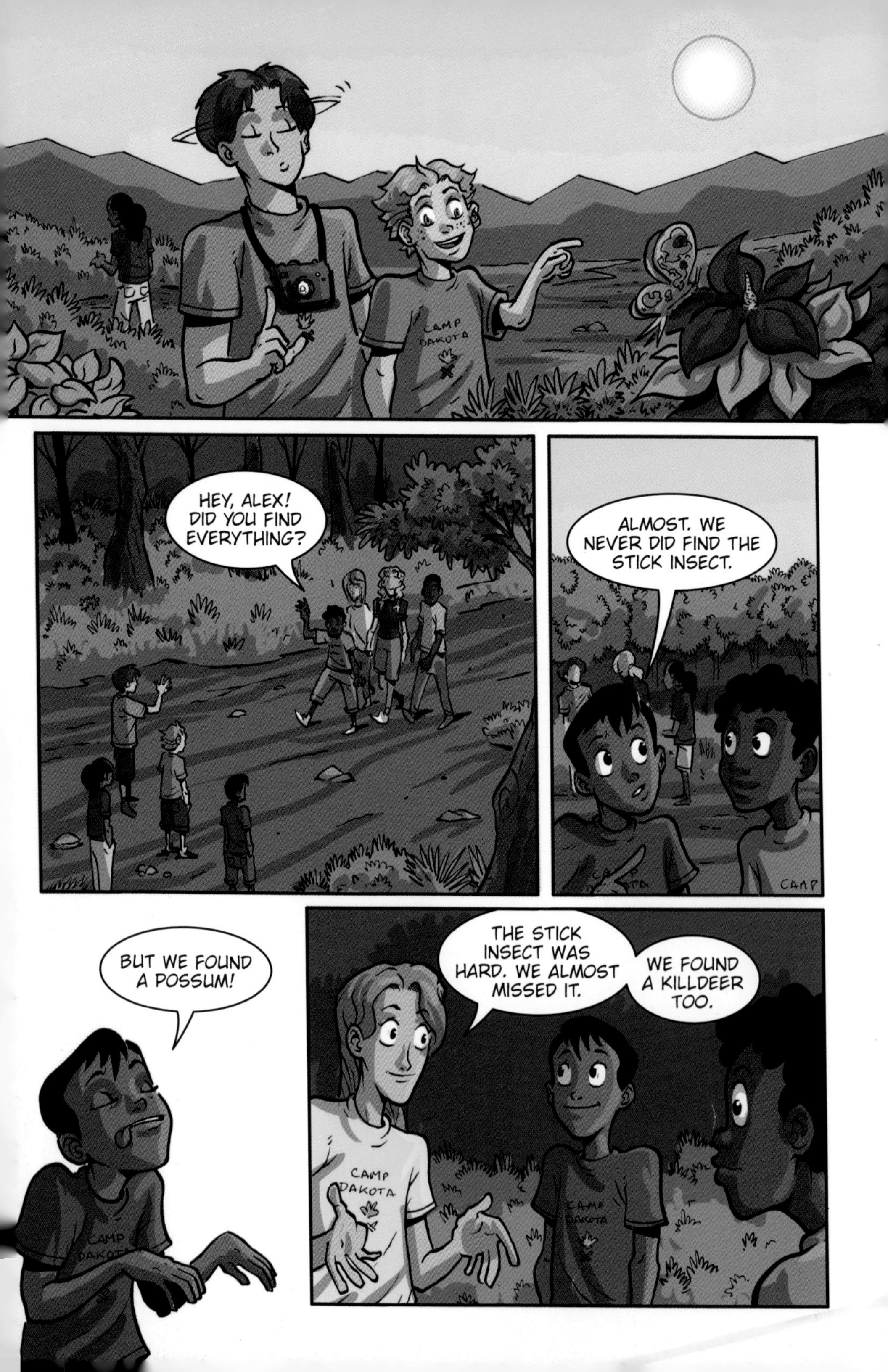
CAMP DAKOTA
HEY, ALEX! DID YOU FIND EVERYTHING?
ALMOST. WE NEVER DID FIND THE STICK INSECT.
CAMP
BUT WE FOUND A POSSUM!
CAMP DAKOTA
THE STICK INSECT WAS HARD. WE ALMOST MISSED IT.
WE FOUND A KILLDEER TOO.
CAMP DAKOTA
CAMP DAKOTA

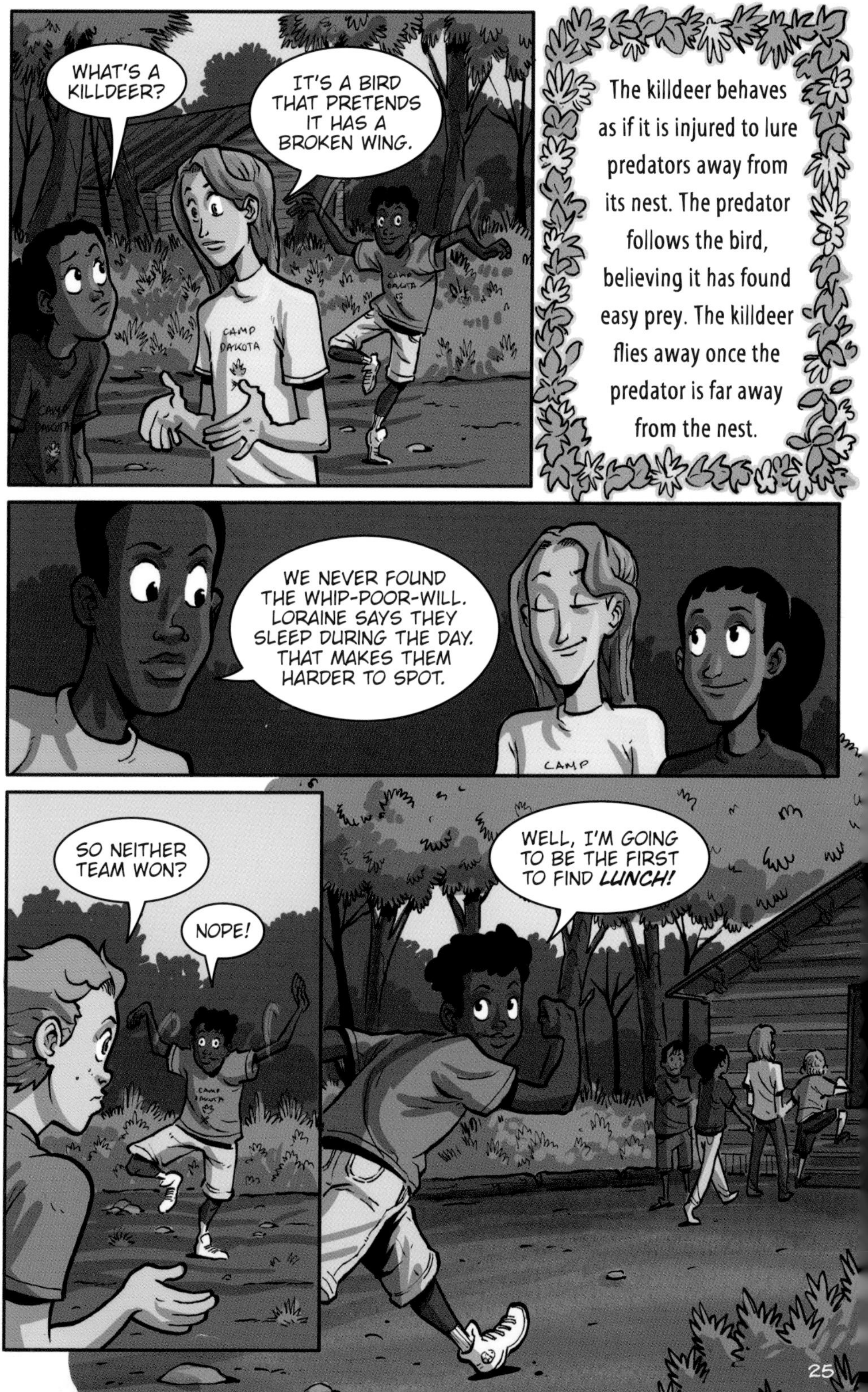
WHAT'S A KILLDEER?
IT'S A BIRD THAT PRETENDS IT HAS A BROKEN WING.
The killdeer behaves as if it is injured to lure predators away from its nest. The predator follows the bird, believing it has found easy prey. The killdeer flies away once the predator is far away from the nest.
WE NEVER FOUND THE WHIP-POOR-WILL. LORAINE SAYS THEY SLEEP DURING THE DAY. THAT MAKES THEM HARDER TO SPOT.
SO NEITHER TEAM WON?
NOPE!
WELL, I'M GOING TO BE THE FIRST TO FIND *LUNCH!*

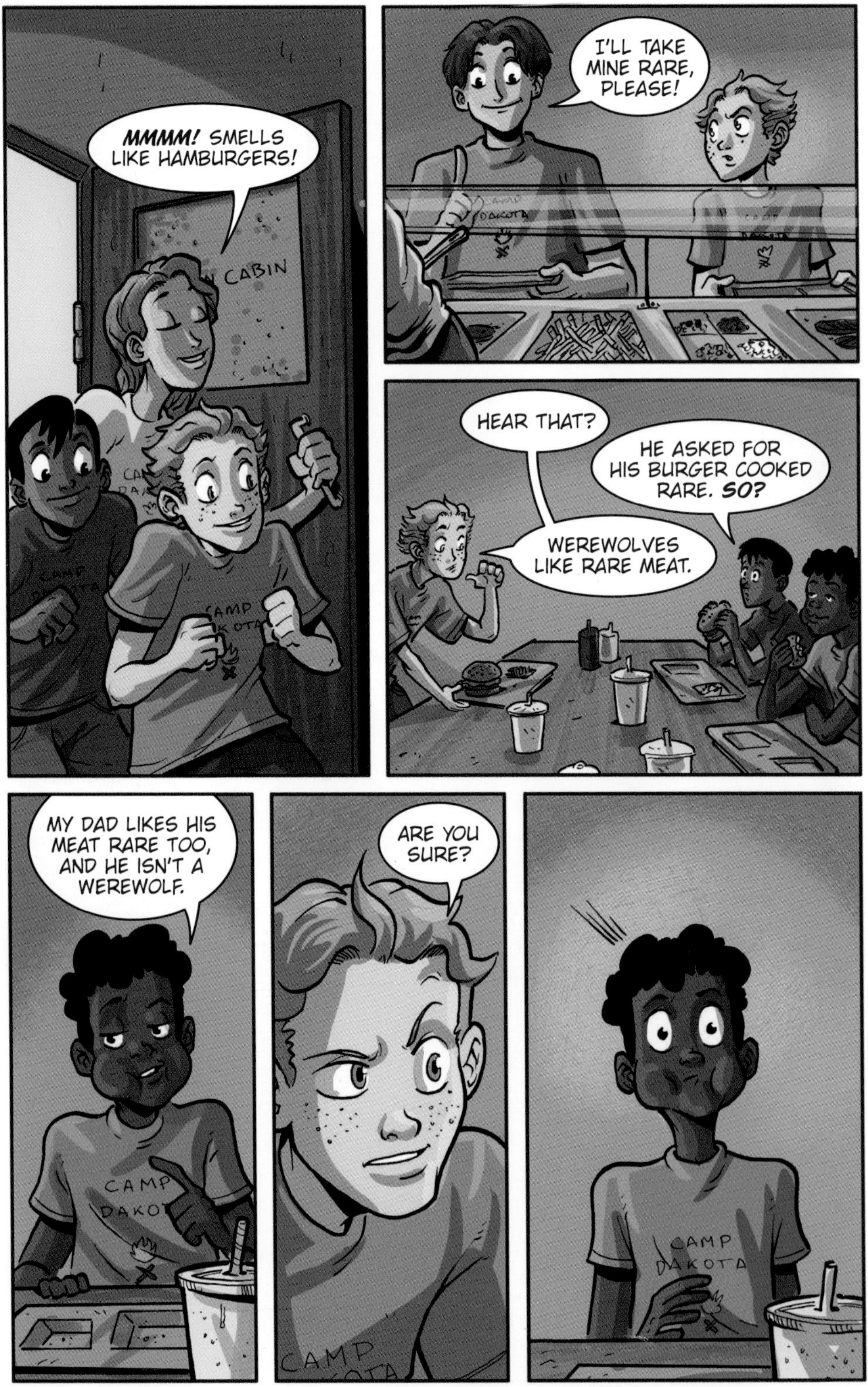
MMMM! SMELLS LIKE HAMBURGERS!
CABIN
I'LL TAKE MINE RARE, PLEASE!
HEAR THAT?
WEREWOLVES LIKE RARE MEAT.
HE ASKED FOR HIS BURGER COOKED RARE. SO?
MY DAD LIKES HIS MEAT RARE TOO, AND HE ISN'T A WEREWOLF.
ARE YOU SURE?

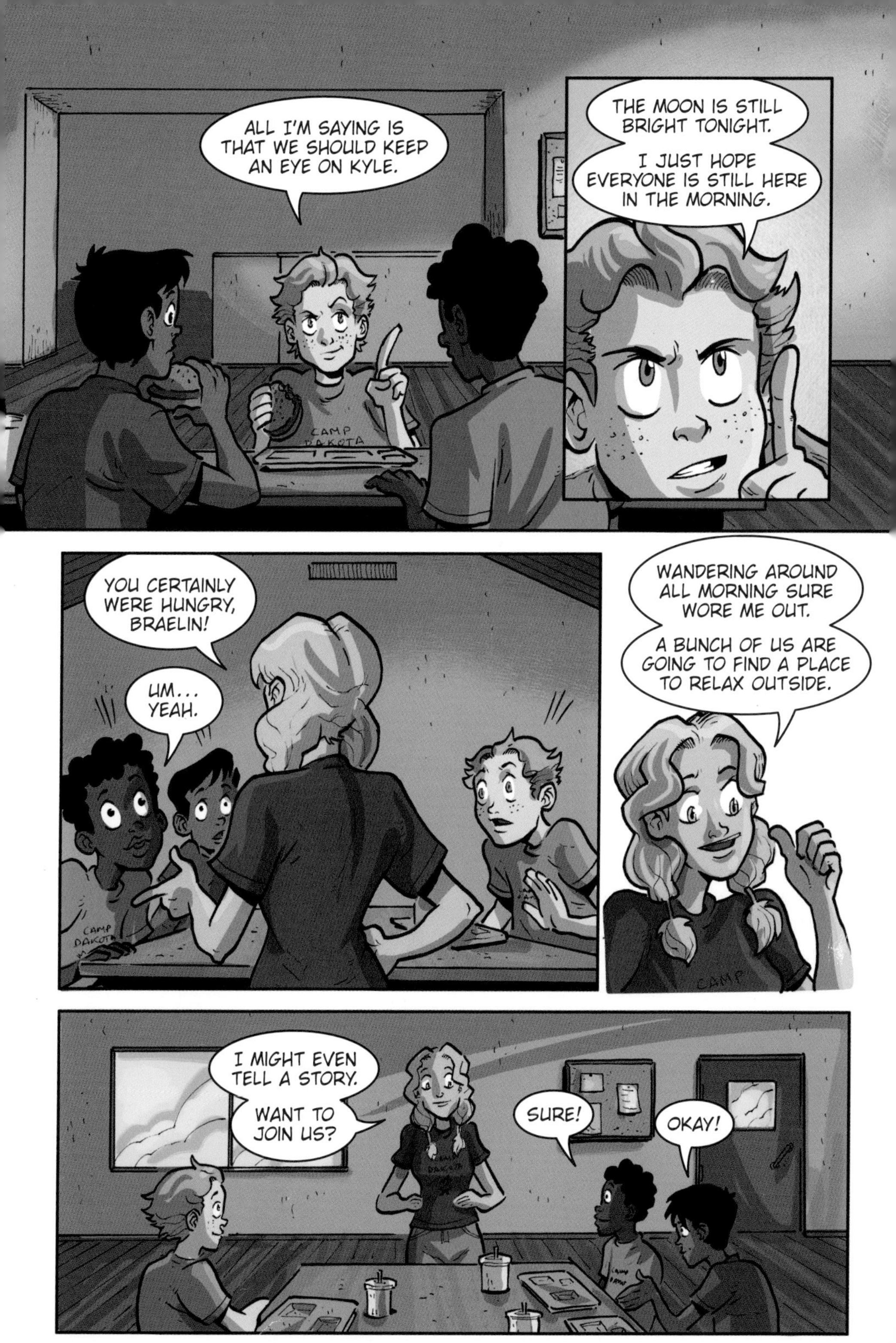

ALL I'M SAYING IS THAT WE SHOULD KEEP AN EYE ON KYLE.
THE MOON IS STILL BRIGHT TONIGHT.
I JUST HOPE EVERYONE IS STILL HERE IN THE MORNING.
CAMP DAKOTA
YOU CERTAINLY WERE HUNGRY, BRAELIN!
UM... YEAH.
WANDERING AROUND ALL MORNING SURE WORE ME OUT.
A BUNCH OF US ARE GOING TO FIND A PLACE TO RELAX OUTSIDE.
CAMP DAKOTA
CAMP
I MIGHT EVEN TELL A STORY.
WANT TO JOIN US?
SURE!
OKAY!

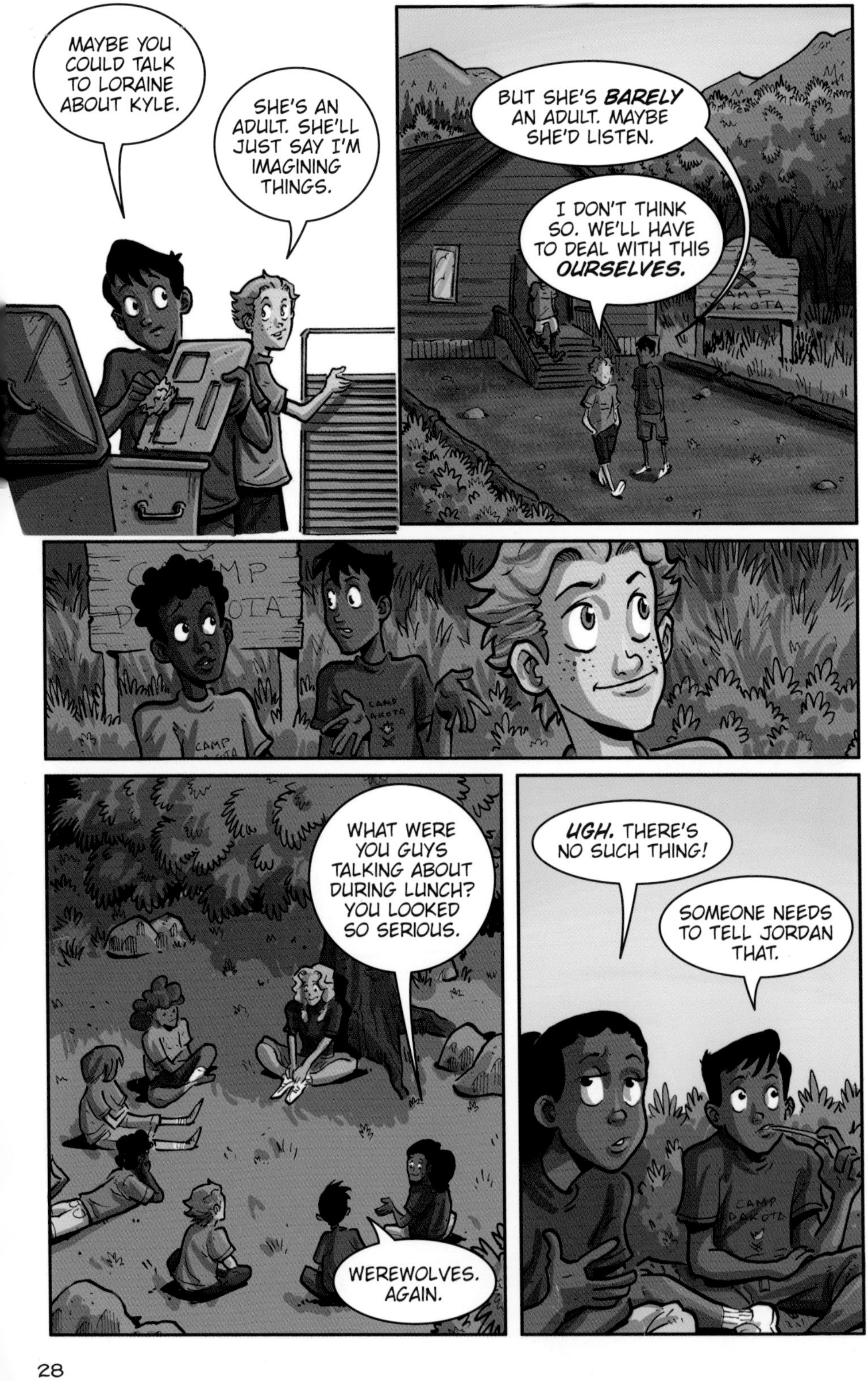
MAYBE YOU COULD TALK TO LORAINE ABOUT KYLE.
SHE'S AN ADULT. SHE'LL JUST SAY I'M IMAGINING THINGS.
BUT SHE'S **BARELY** AN ADULT. MAYBE SHE'D LISTEN.
I DON'T THINK SO. WE'LL HAVE TO DEAL WITH THIS **OURSELVES.**
CAMP DAKOTA
WHAT WERE YOU GUYS TALKING ABOUT DURING LUNCH? YOU LOOKED SO SERIOUS.
WEREWOLVES. AGAIN.
UGH. THERE'S NO SUCH THING!
SOMEONE NEEDS TO TELL JORDAN THAT.

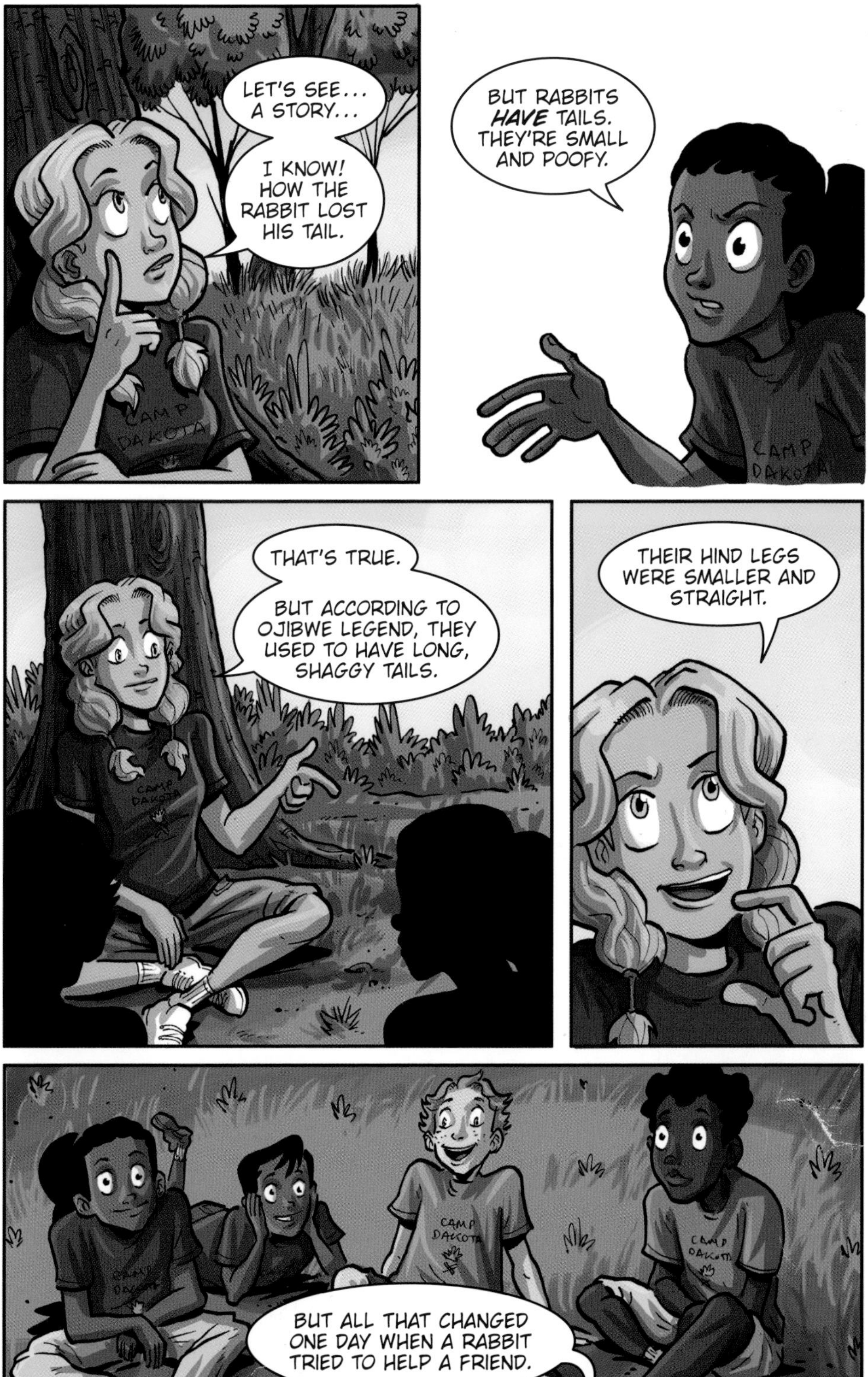
LET'S SEE... A STORY...
I KNOW! HOW THE RABBIT LOST HIS TAIL.
BUT RABBITS HAVE TAILS. THEY'RE SMALL AND POOFY.
CAMP DAKOTA
THAT'S TRUE.
BUT ACCORDING TO OJIBWE LEGEND, THEY USED TO HAVE LONG, SHAGGY TAILS.
THEIR HIND LEGS WERE SMALLER AND STRAIGHT.
BUT ALL THAT CHANGED ONE DAY WHEN A RABBIT TRIED TO HELP A FRIEND.

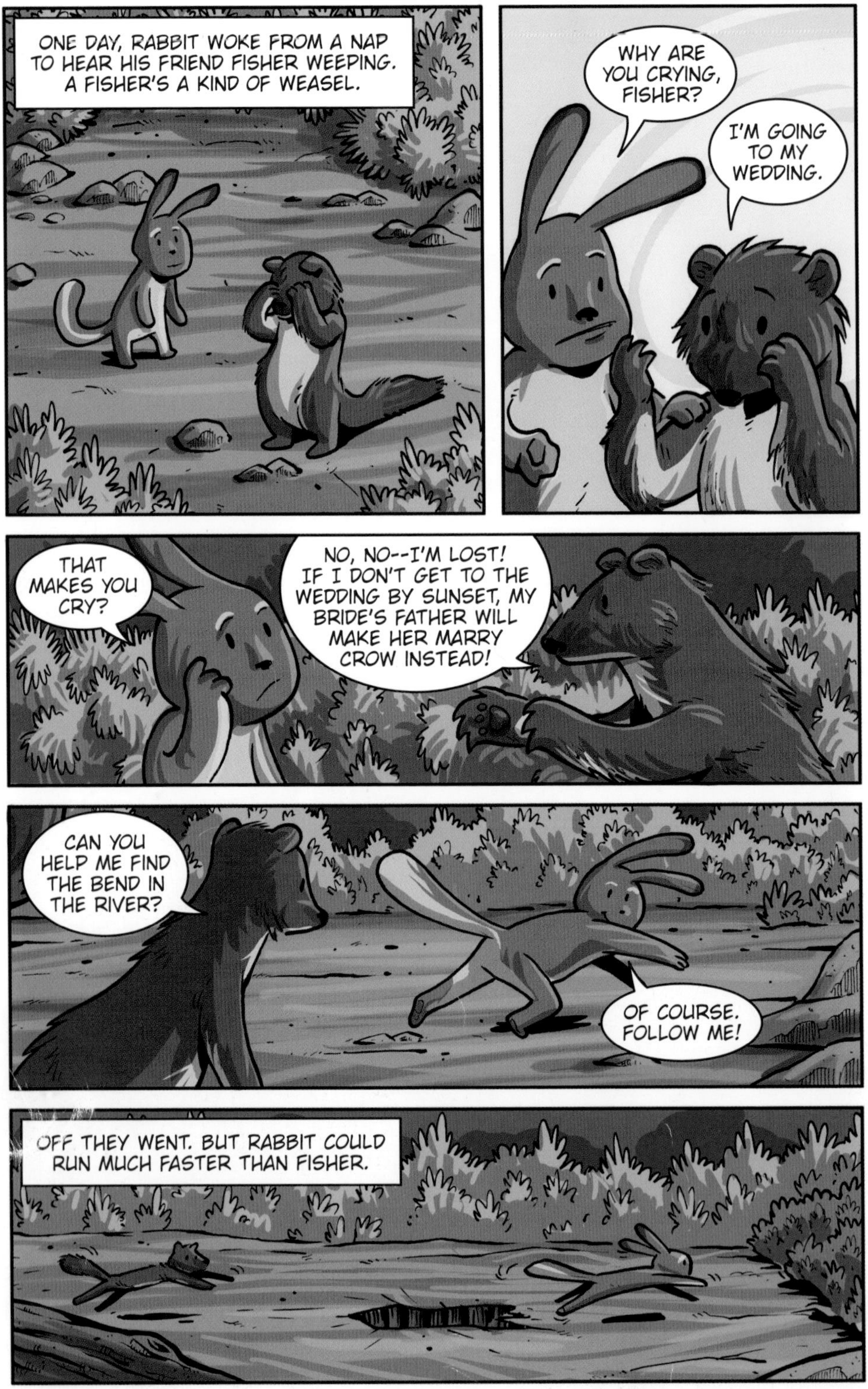
ONE DAY, RABBIT WOKE FROM A NAP TO HEAR HIS FRIEND FISHER WEEPING. A FISHER'S A KIND OF WEASEL.
WHY ARE YOU CRYING, FISHER?
I'M GOING TO MY WEDDING.
THAT MAKES YOU CRY?
NO, NO--I'M LOST! IF I DON'T GET TO THE WEDDING BY SUNSET, MY BRIDE'S FATHER WILL MAKE HER MARRY CROW INSTEAD!
CAN YOU HELP ME FIND THE BEND IN THE RIVER?
OF COURSE. FOLLOW ME!
OFF THEY WENT. BUT RABBIT COULD RUN MUCH FASTER THAN FISHER.

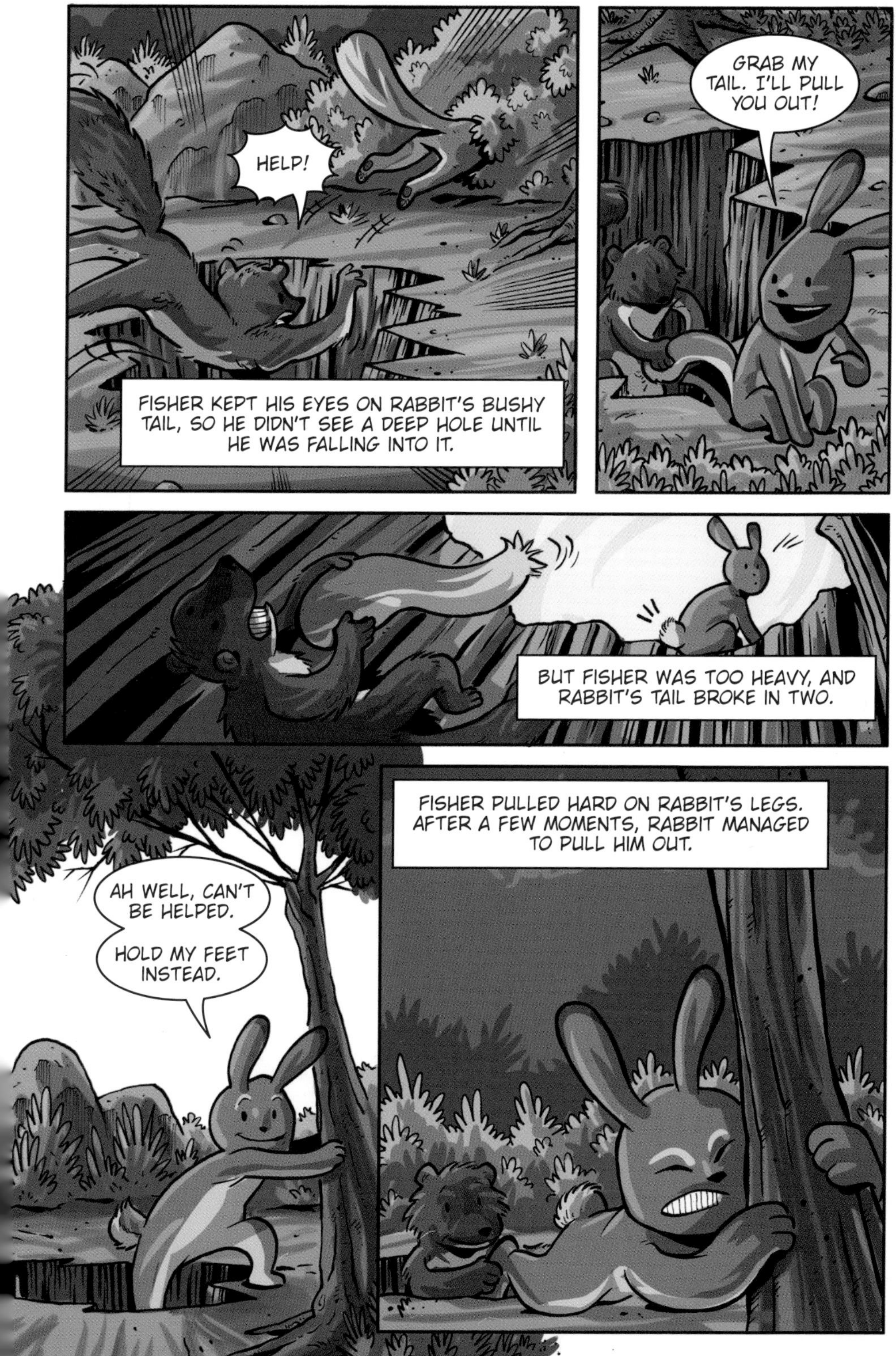
HELP!
FISHER KEPT HIS EYES ON RABBIT'S BUSHY TAIL, SO HE DIDN'T SEE A DEEP HOLE UNTIL HE WAS FALLING INTO IT.
GRAB MY TAIL. I'LL PULL YOU OUT!
BUT FISHER WAS TOO HEAVY, AND RABBIT'S TAIL BROKE IN TWO.
AH WELL, CAN'T BE HELPED.
HOLD MY FEET INSTEAD.
FISHER PULLED HARD ON RABBIT'S LEGS. AFTER A FEW MOMENTS, RABBIT MANAGED TO PULL HIM OUT.

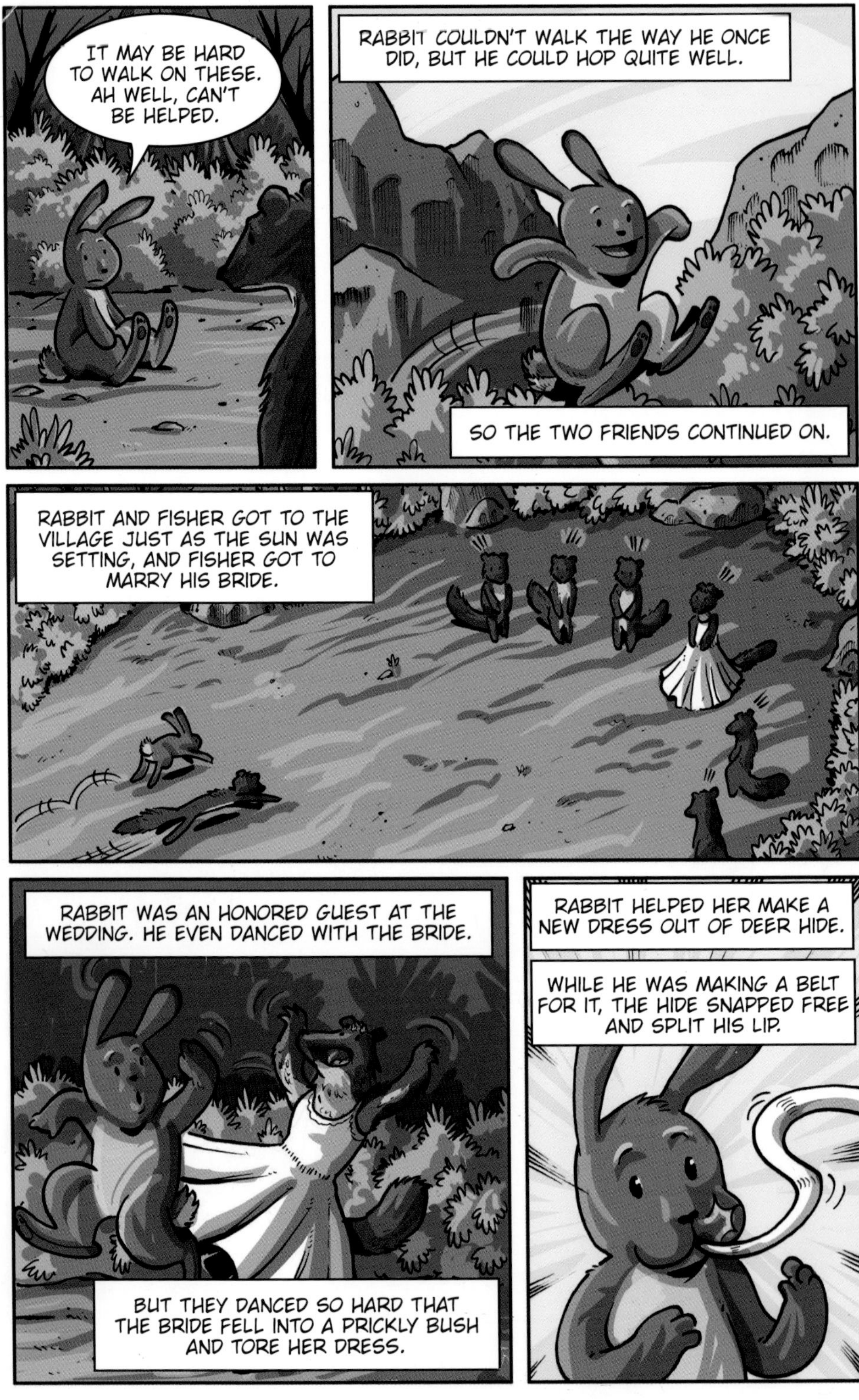
IT MAY BE HARD TO WALK ON THESE. AH WELL, CAN'T BE HELPED.
RABBIT COULDN'T WALK THE WAY HE ONCE DID, BUT HE COULD HOP QUITE WELL.
SO THE TWO FRIENDS CONTINUED ON.
RABBIT AND FISHER GOT TO THE VILLAGE JUST AS THE SUN WAS SETTING, AND FISHER GOT TO MARRY HIS BRIDE.
RABBIT WAS AN HONORED GUEST AT THE WEDDING. HE EVEN DANCED WITH THE BRIDE.
BUT THEY DANCED SO HARD THAT THE BRIDE FELL INTO A PRICKLY BUSH AND TORE HER DRESS.
RABBIT HELPED HER MAKE A NEW DRESS OUT OF DEER HIDE.
WHILE HE WAS MAKING A BELT FOR IT, THE HIDE SNAPPED FREE AND SPLIT HIS LIP.

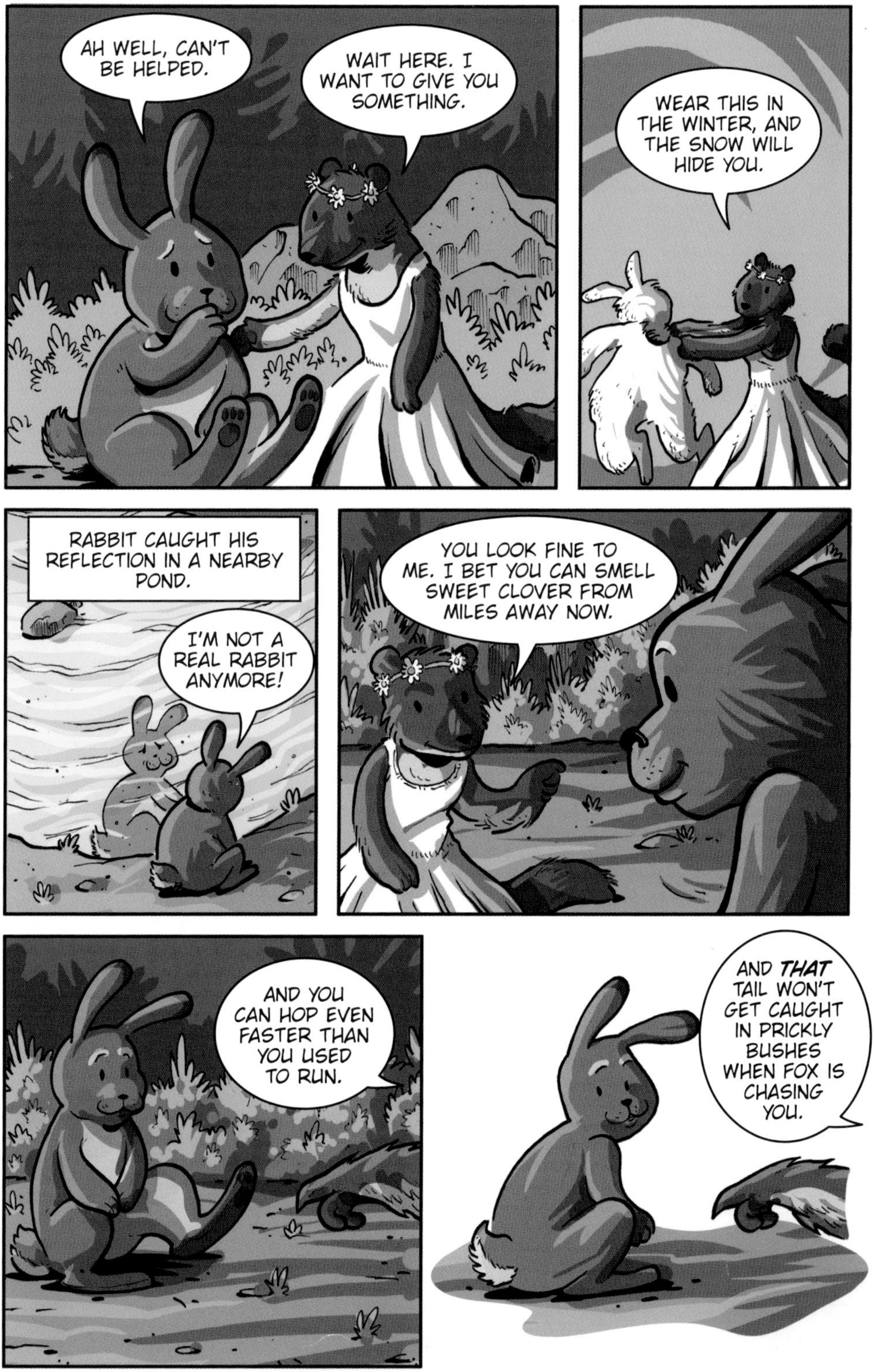
AH WELL, CAN'T BE HELPED.
WAIT HERE. I WANT TO GIVE YOU SOMETHING.
WEAR THIS IN THE WINTER, AND THE SNOW WILL HIDE YOU.
RABBIT CAUGHT HIS REFLECTION IN A NEARBY POND.
I'M NOT A REAL RABBIT ANYMORE!
YOU LOOK FINE TO ME. I BET YOU CAN SMELL SWEET CLOVER FROM MILES AWAY NOW.
AND YOU CAN HOP EVEN FASTER THAN YOU USED TO RUN.
AND ***THAT*** TAIL WON'T GET CAUGHT IN PRICKLY BUSHES WHEN FOX IS CHASING YOU.

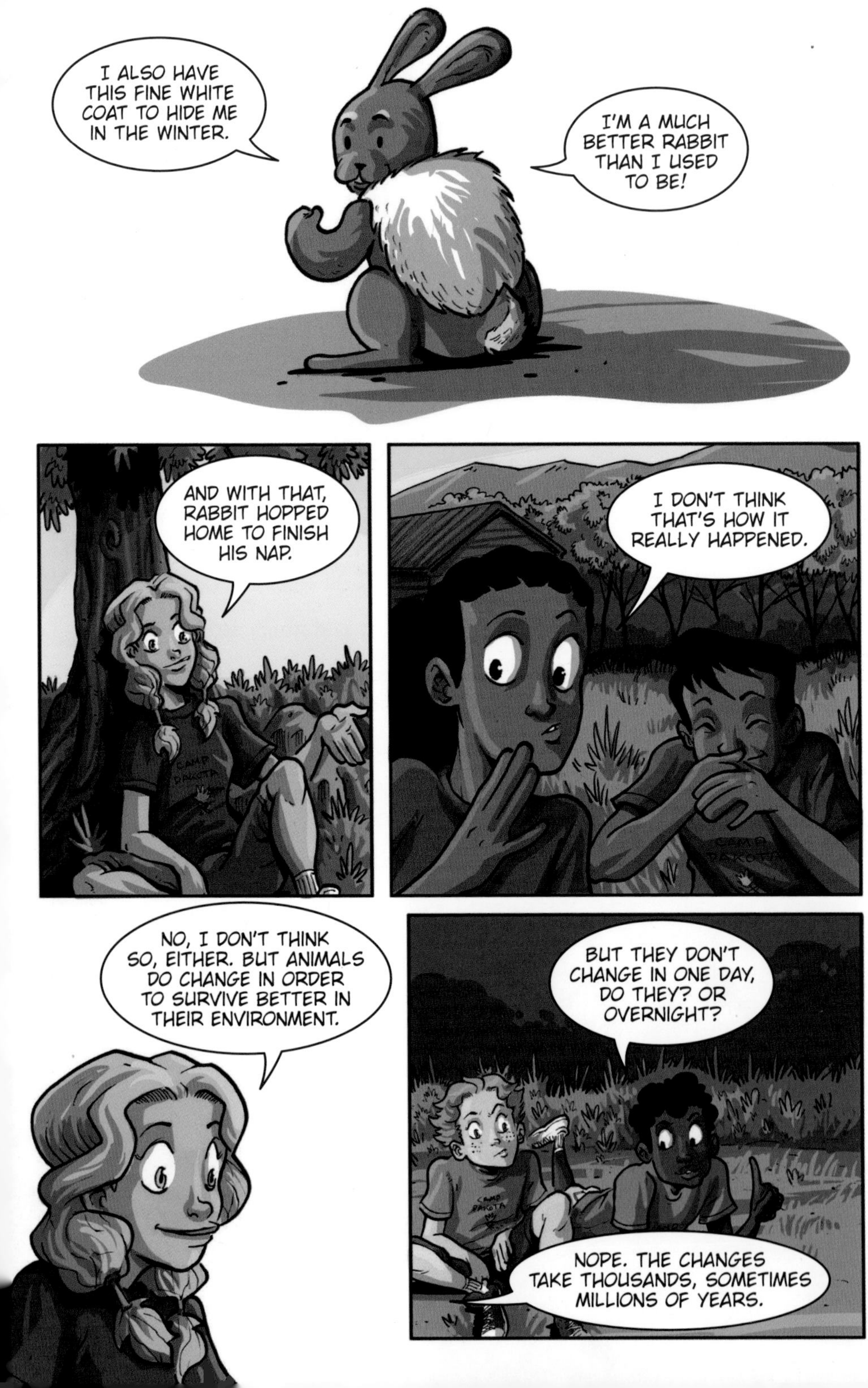
I ALSO HAVE THIS FINE WHITE COAT TO HIDE ME IN THE WINTER.
I'M A MUCH BETTER RABBIT THAN I USED TO BE!
AND WITH THAT, RABBIT HOPPED HOME TO FINISH HIS NAP.
I DON'T THINK THAT'S HOW IT REALLY HAPPENED.
NO, I DON'T THINK SO, EITHER. BUT ANIMALS DO CHANGE IN ORDER TO SURVIVE BETTER IN THEIR ENVIRONMENT.
BUT THEY DON'T CHANGE IN ONE DAY, DO THEY? OR OVERNIGHT?
NOPE. THE CHANGES TAKE THOUSANDS, SOMETIMES MILLIONS OF YEARS.

IN MONGOLIA'S GOBI DESERT, SCIENTISTS HAVE FOUND A 55-MILLION-YEAR-OLD FOSSIL THAT MAY HAVE BEEN AN EARLY FORM OF RABBIT. THIS ANIMAL, CALLED *GOMPHOS ELKEMA*, HAD HIND LEGS THAT WERE TWICE AS LONG AS ITS FRONT LEGS. THESE LONG LEGS LIKELY HELPED IT TO HOP AND BOUND, JUST LIKE THE HIND LEGS OF MODERN-DAY RABBITS.

UNLIKE MODERN RABBIT, *GOMPHOS ELKEMA* HAD SHORT EARS AND A LONG TAIL. THESE TRAITS MAY HAVE CHANGED AS THE ENVIRONMENT AROUND THE ANIMAL CHANGED--IN THIS CASE, AS TEMPERATURES INCREASED AND MORE PREDATORS CAME TO THE AREA. THE LONG EARS OF MODERN RABBITS GIVE OFF HEAT SO THE RABBITS CAN STAY COOL. THEY ALSO ALLOW RABBITS TO HEAR FAINT OR FARAWAY NOISES AND AVOID THE ANIMALS THAT HUNT THEM.

KANGAROOS HAVE LONG HIND LEGS, LIKE *GOMPHOS ELKEMA* AND MODERN RABBITS. BUT KANGAROOS HOP ON TWO LEGS INSTEAD OF FOUR, SO THEY NEED A LONG TAIL FOR BALANCE. SINCE RABBITS STAY LOW AND BOUND ON ALL FOUR LEGS, A LONG TAIL ISN'T NECESSARY-- AND RABBIT TAILS SEEM TO HAVE SHRUNK OVER TIME.

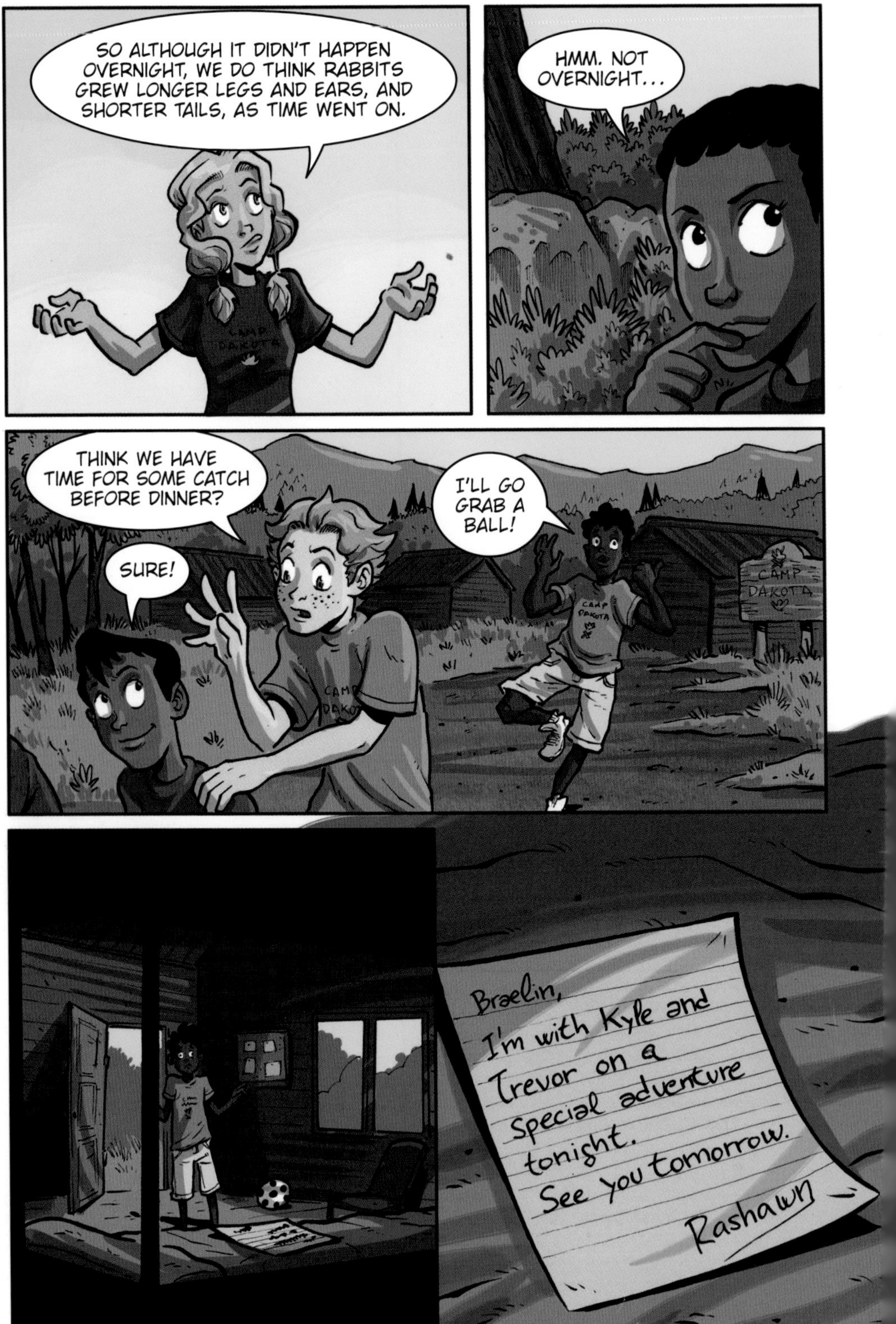
SO ALTHOUGH IT DIDN'T HAPPEN OVERNIGHT, WE DO THINK RABBITS GREW LONGER LEGS AND EARS, AND SHORTER TAILS, AS TIME WENT ON.
HMM. NOT OVERNIGHT...
CAMP DAKOTA
THINK WE HAVE TIME FOR SOME CATCH BEFORE DINNER?
SURE!
I'LL GO GRAB A BALL!
CAMP DAKOTA
Braelin,
I'm with Kyle and Trevor on a Special adventure tonight.
See you tomorrow.
Rashawn

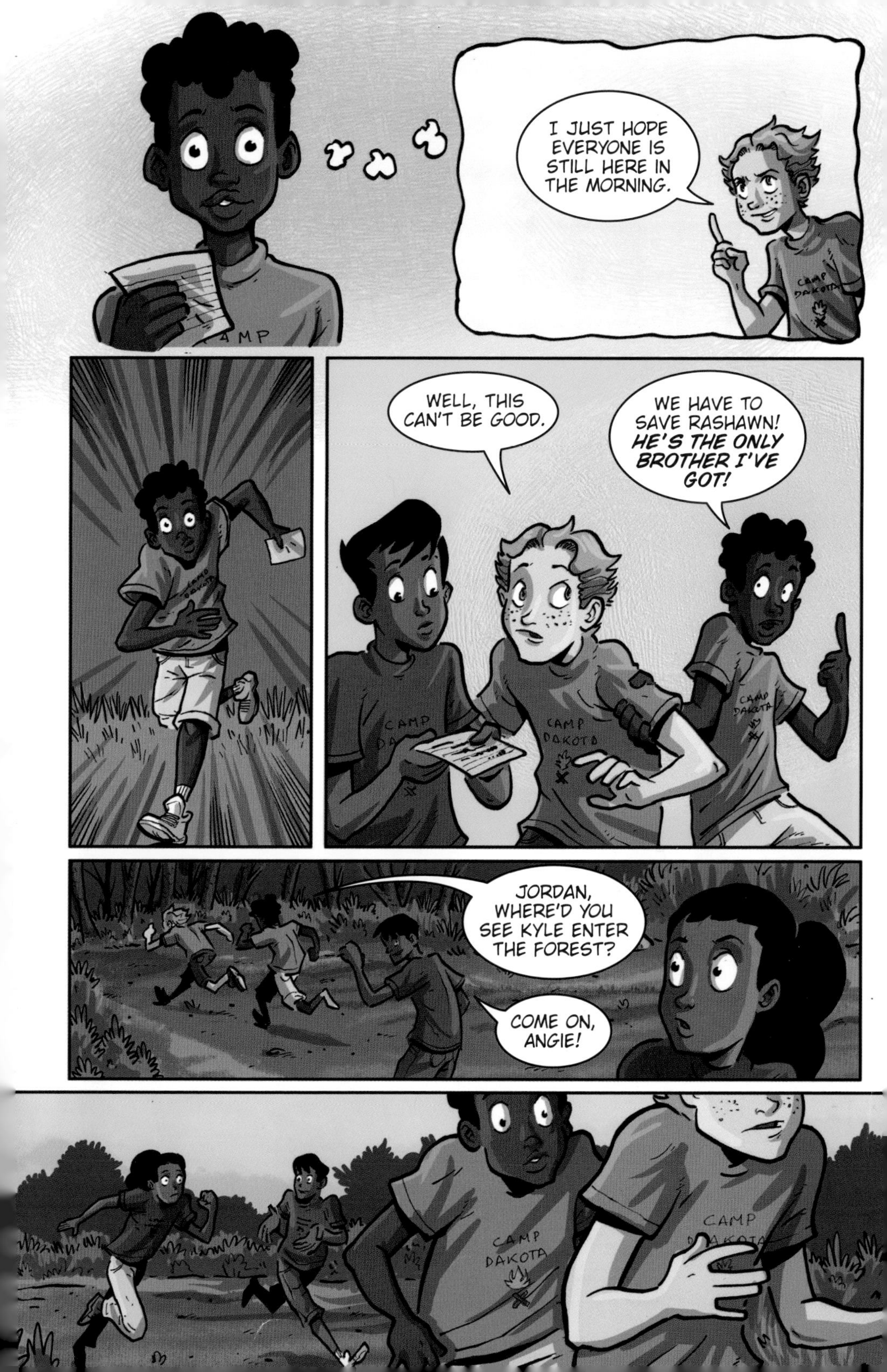
I JUST HOPE EVERYONE IS STILL HERE IN THE MORNING.
WELL, THIS CAN'T BE GOOD.
WE HAVE TO SAVE RASHAWN! ***HE'S THE ONLY BROTHER I'VE GOT!***
JORDAN, WHERE'D YOU SEE KYLE ENTER THE FOREST?
COME ON, ANGIE!

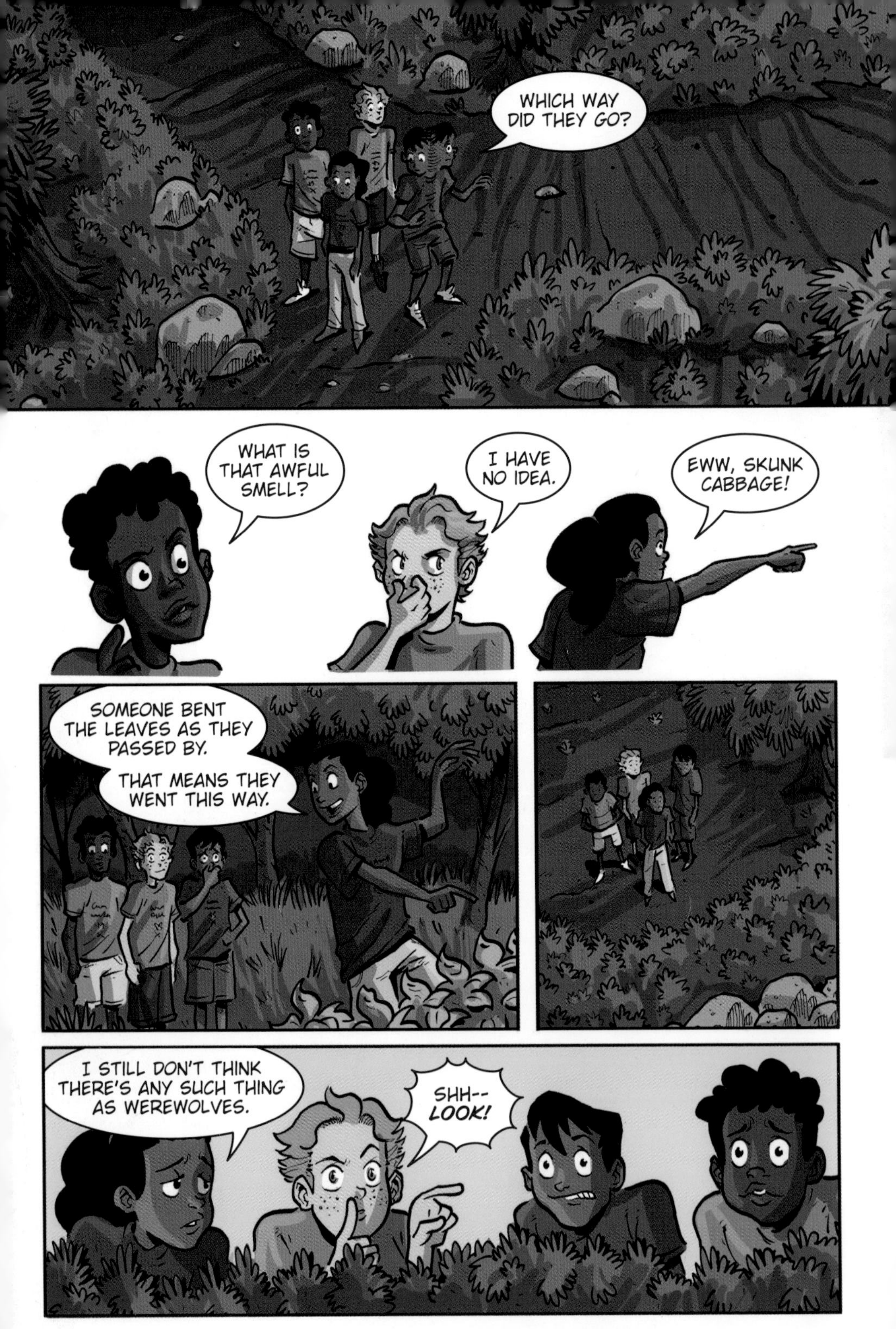

WHICH WAY DID THEY GO?
WHAT IS THAT AWFUL SMELL?
I HAVE NO IDEA.
EWW, SKUNK CABBAGE!
SOMEONE BENT THE LEAVES AS THEY PASSED BY.
THAT MEANS THEY WENT THIS WAY.
I STILL DON'T THINK THERE'S ANY SUCH THING AS WEREWOLVES.
SHH-- *LOOK!*

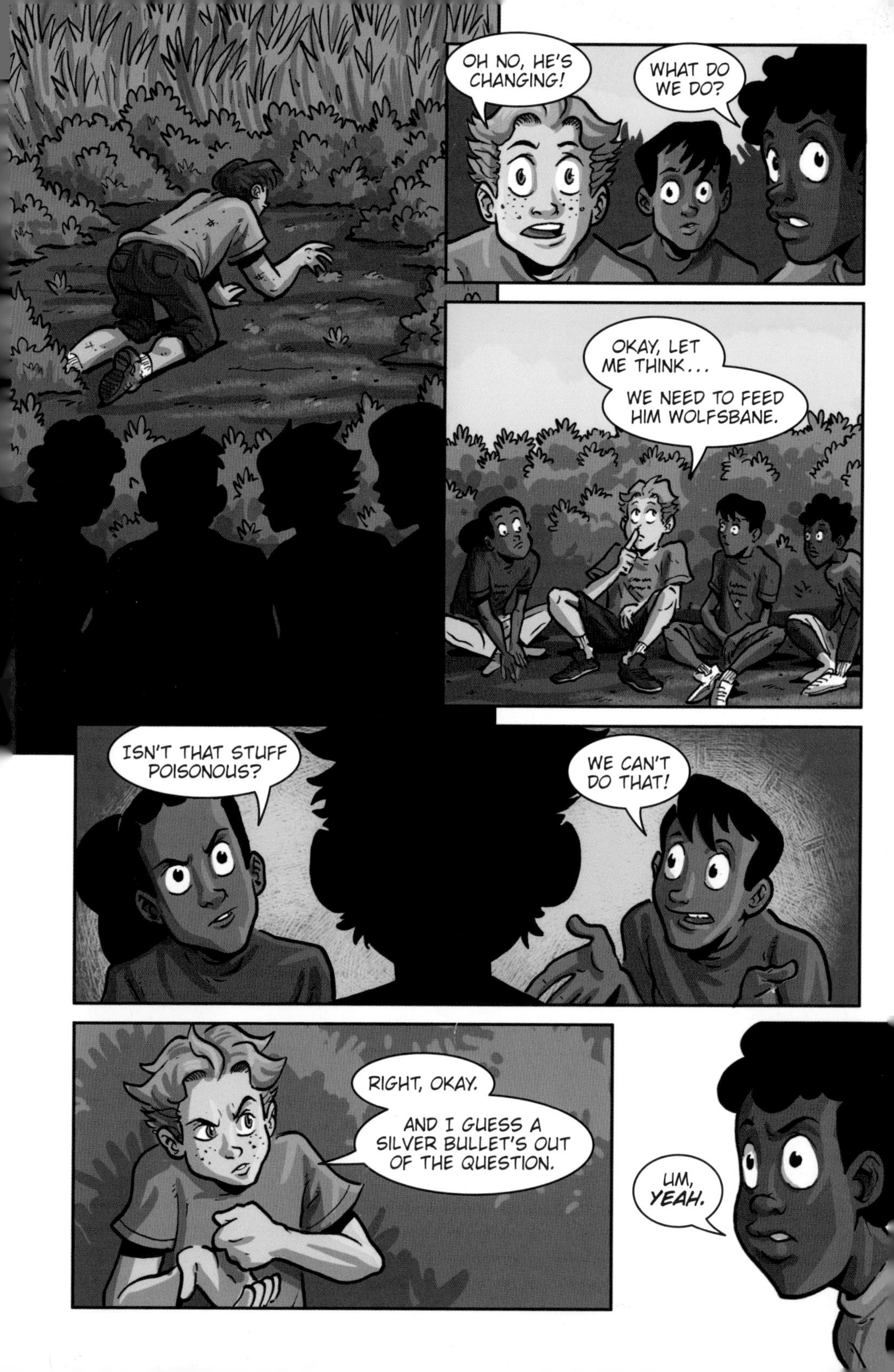
OH NO, HE'S CHANGING!
WHAT DO WE DO?
OKAY, LET ME THINK...
WE NEED TO FEED HIM WOLFSBANE.
ISN'T THAT STUFF POISONOUS?
WE CAN'T DO THAT!
RIGHT, OKAY.
AND I GUESS A SILVER BULLET'S OUT OF THE QUESTION.
UM, YEAH.

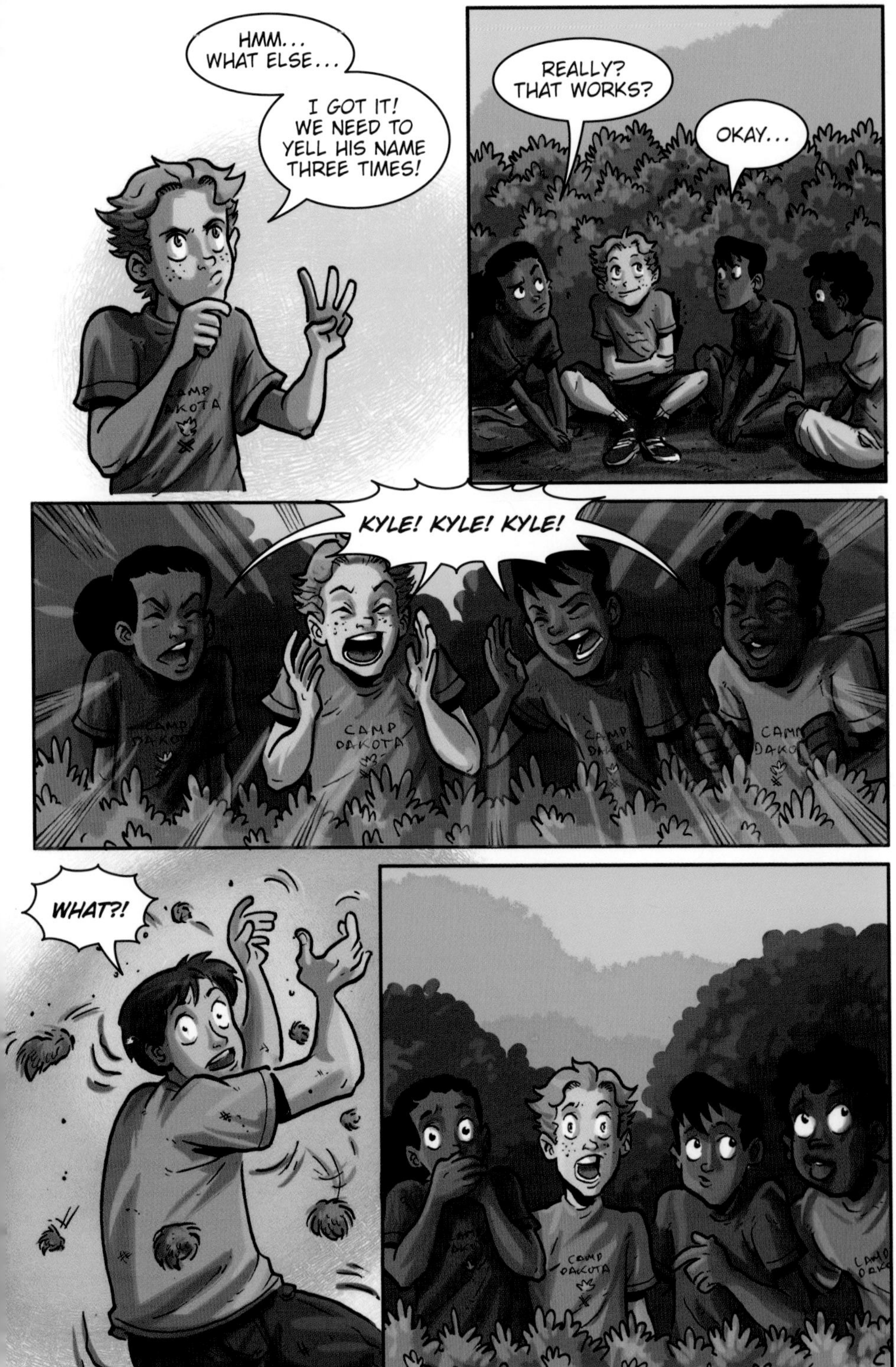
HMM... WHAT ELSE...
I GOT IT! WE NEED TO YELL HIS NAME THREE TIMES!
REALLY? THAT WORKS?
OKAY...
KYLE! KYLE! KYLE!
WHAT?!

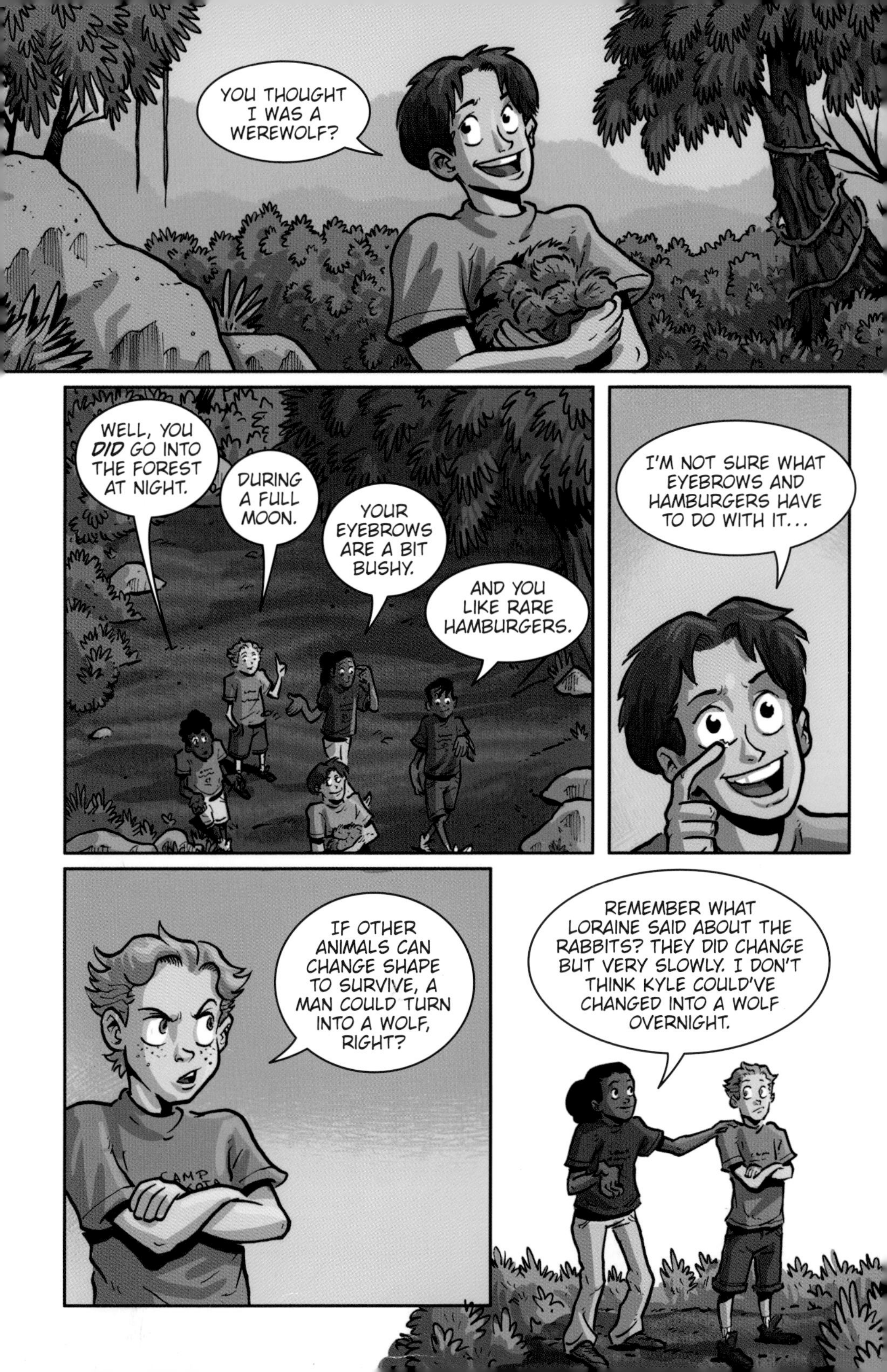
YOU THOUGHT I WAS A WEREWOLF?
WELL, YOU *DID* GO INTO THE FOREST AT NIGHT.
DURING A FULL MOON.
YOUR EYEBROWS ARE A BIT BUSHY.
AND YOU LIKE RARE HAMBURGERS.
I'M NOT SURE WHAT EYEBROWS AND HAMBURGERS HAVE TO DO WITH IT...
IF OTHER ANIMALS CAN CHANGE SHAPE TO SURVIVE, A MAN COULD TURN INTO A WOLF, RIGHT?
REMEMBER WHAT LORAINE SAID ABOUT THE RABBITS? THEY DID CHANGE BUT VERY SLOWLY. I DON'T THINK KYLE COULD'VE CHANGED INTO A WOLF OVERNIGHT.

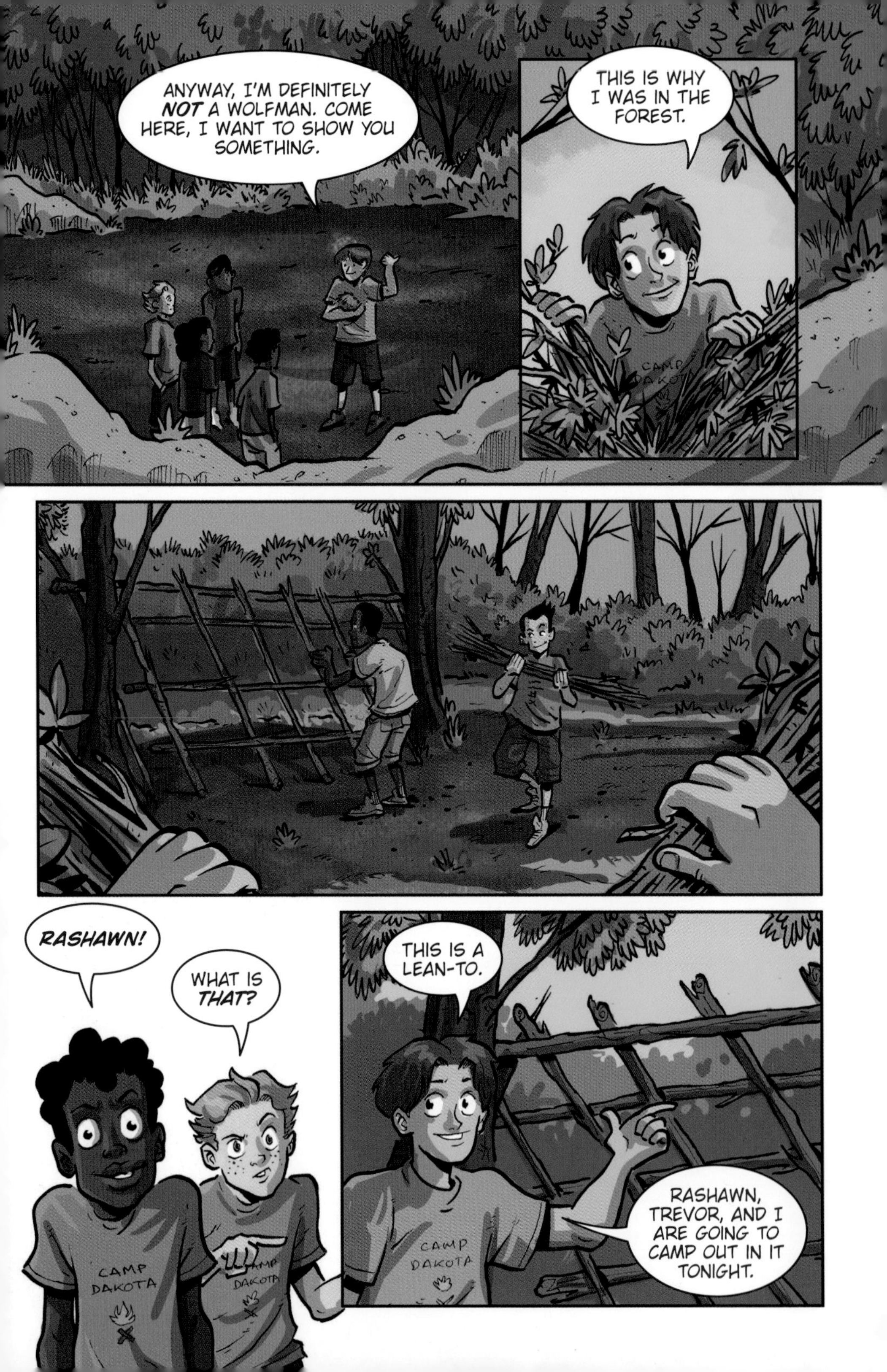
ANYWAY, I'M DEFINITELY NOT A WOLFMAN. COME HERE, I WANT TO SHOW YOU SOMETHING.
THIS IS WHY I WAS IN THE FOREST.
CAMP DAKOTA
RASHAWN!
WHAT IS THAT?
CAMP DAKOTA
CAMP DAKOTA
THIS IS A LEAN-TO.
CAMP DAKOTA
RASHAWN, TREVOR, AND I ARE GOING TO CAMP OUT IN IT TONIGHT.

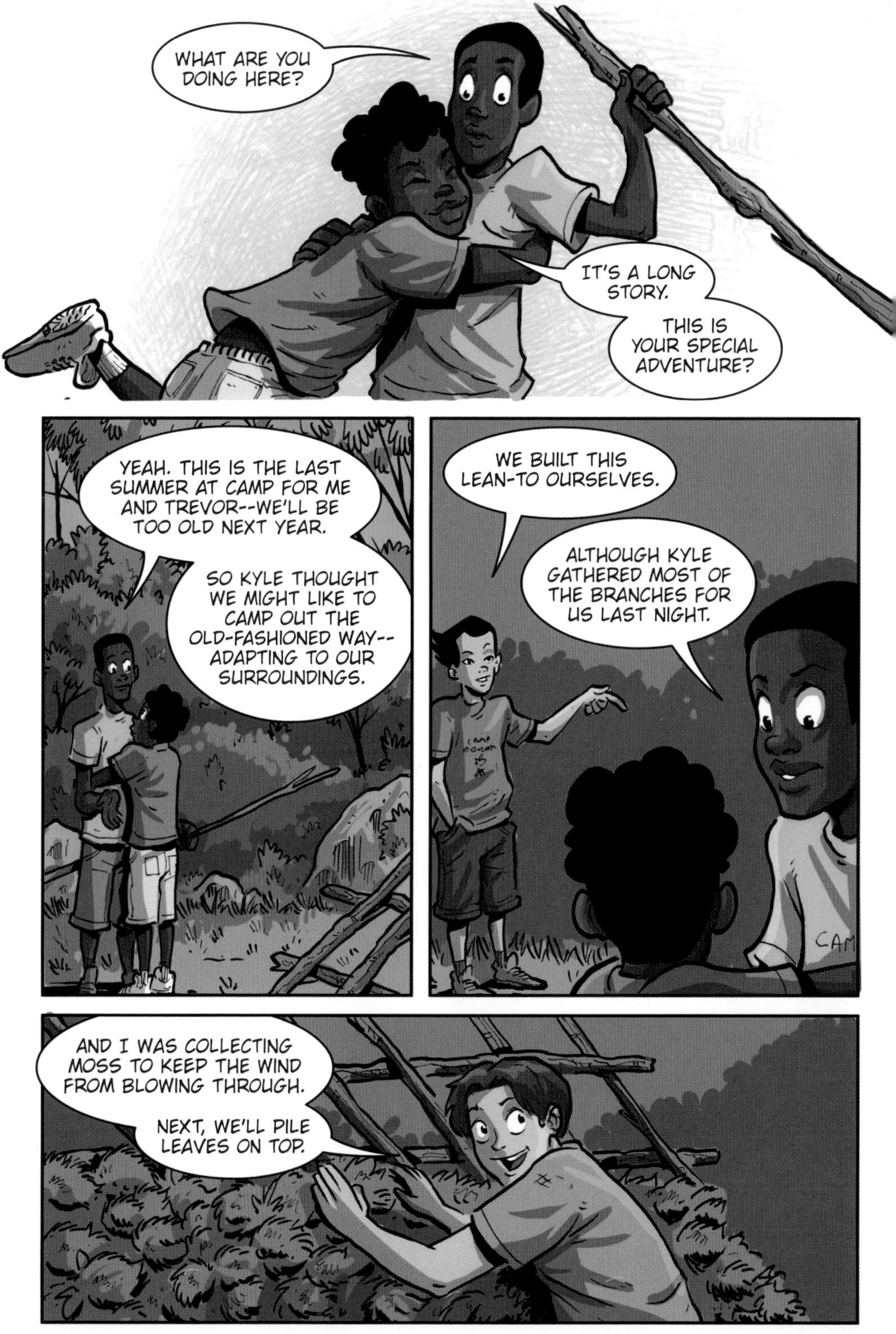
WHAT ARE YOU DOING HERE?
IT'S A LONG STORY.
THIS IS YOUR SPECIAL ADVENTURE?
YEAH. THIS IS THE LAST SUMMER AT CAMP FOR ME AND TREVOR--WE'LL BE TOO OLD NEXT YEAR.
SO KYLE THOUGHT WE MIGHT LIKE TO CAMP OUT THE OLD-FASHIONED WAY--ADAPTING TO OUR SURROUNDINGS.
WE BUILT THIS LEAN-TO OURSELVES.
ALTHOUGH KYLE GATHERED MOST OF THE BRANCHES FOR US LAST NIGHT.
AND I WAS COLLECTING MOSS TO KEEP THE WIND FROM BLOWING THROUGH.
NEXT, WE'LL PILE LEAVES ON TOP.

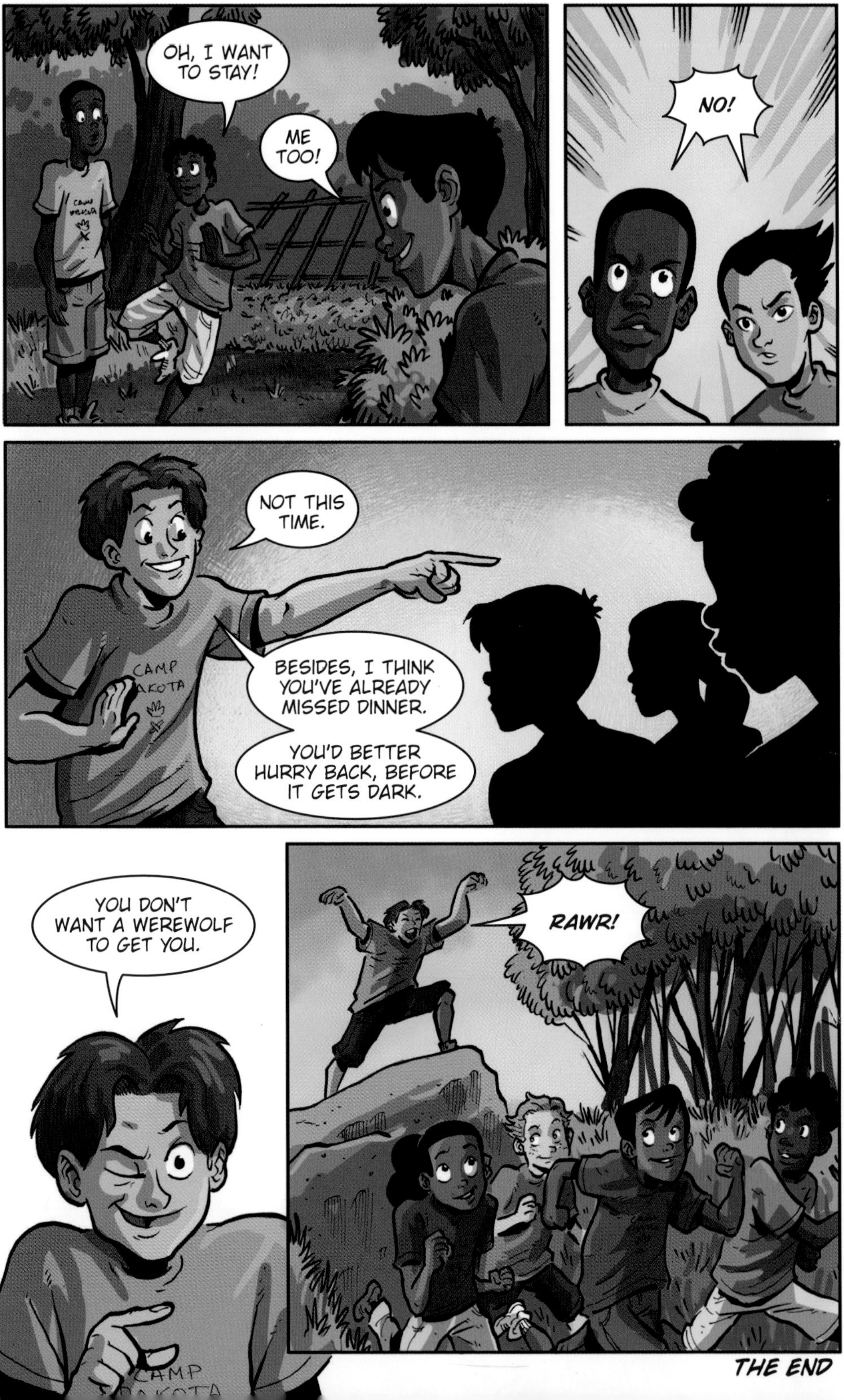
OH, I WANT TO STAY!
ME TOO!
NO!
NOT THIS TIME.
BESIDES, I THINK YOU'VE ALREADY MISSED DINNER.
YOU'D BETTER HURRY BACK, BEFORE IT GETS DARK.
YOU DON'T WANT A WEREWOLF TO GET YOU.
RAWR!
THE END

Experiments

Try these fun experiments at home or in your classroom.
Make sure you have an adult help out.

Eat Like a Bird

You will need: jar or cup, sand, berries, nuts, raisins, seeds, cooked spaghetti, coffee grounds, leaves, pliers, nutcracker, drinking straw, tweezers, sieve or strainer, and tape

1. Spread out the tools on one side of the table and the food on the other side. Fill the jar with sand, and bury a few strands of spaghetti in it, making "worms." Cover the coffee grounds with leaves, and pretend they are insects.

2. Take each tool one at a time and try to pick up the various food items. Which tools work best with which foods?

How does it work?

Bird beaks are designed to help each species of bird collect and eat the types of food found in its native environment. Some beaks can work with a wide variety of foods, while others are very specialized. Cone-shaped bills (similar to the nutcracker) are used for cracking seeds. Thin, pointed beaks (similar to the tweezers) are good for picking insects off leaves and bark. Hummingbird beaks (similar to the straw) are suited to sipping nectar out of flowers.

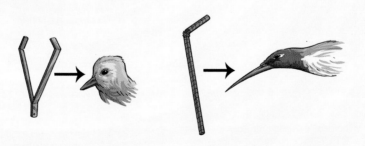

Head for the Light

This experiment takes a little while, so be patient!

You will need: small plastic cups or pots, potting soil, sunflower seeds, permanent marker, ruler, fluorescent light, and sunny window

1. Fill the cups or pots with potting soil. Plant the sunflower seeds in the soil.

2. Water the soil, then place the pots directly under a fluorescent light.

3. Water them again when they get dry. Let them grow until they have several leaves.

4. Using the marker, put an *A* on one side of each pot and a *B* on the other.

5. Mark the leaves on both the A and B sides with dots. Put one dot on each of the leaves on the level closest to the pot, then two dots on the next leaves up, and so on.

6. Measure and write down the distance from each set of leaves to the bottom of the pot.

7. Take half the plants and put them in a sunny window, with the A side facing the window.

8. Wait two days, and then measure and write down the distance again, measuring both the A and B side leaves.

9. Repeat the measurements again two days later, then again two days after that.

10. Compare the measurements between the sunny-window plants and the overhead-light plants.

What happened?

When one side of a plant doesn't get enough light, the plant adapts to the situation by releasing a chemical. The chemical makes the cells on the dark side of the plant grow longer. This makes the plant bend toward the light.

Mysterious Words

adaptation: a change in the structure or behavior of an organism that helps it survive in its environment

camouflage: a disguise or a coloring that hides an organism by allowing it to blend in with its surroundings

climate: the conditions of an environment such as temperature, precipitation, and wind

insulation: a material or substance used to prevent the passage of heat in or out of a space

mammal: a warm-blooded animal that nourishes its young with milk and typically has hair on its skin

pollinate: to transfer pollen from one plant to another

Could YOU have solved the mystery of the Camp Dakota werewolf?

Good thing the kids of Camp Dakota knew a bit about adaptations. See if you caught all the facts they put to use.

- Animals—including people—adapt to their environments in order to survive.

- A physical adaptation means a change to an animal's body. A behavior adaptation means a change in the way an animal lives its life.

- A behavior adaptation can take place all at once (although some habits are hard to break). But a physical adaptation can take hundreds, thousands, or even millions of years.

THE AUTHOR

LYNDA BEAUREGARD wrote her first story when she was seven years old and hasn't stopped writing since. She also likes teaching kids how to swim, designing websites, directing race cars out onto the track, and throwing bouncy balls for her cat, Becca. She lives near Detroit, Michigan, with her two lovely daughters, who are doing their best to turn her hair gray.

THE ARTISTS

DER-SHING HELMER graduated from University of California—Berkeley, where she played with snakes and lizards all summer long. When she is not teaching biology to high school students, she is making art and comics for everyone to enjoy. Her best friends are her two pet geckos (Smeg and Jerry), her king snake (Clarice), and the chinchilla that lives next door.

GUILLERMO MOGORRÓN started drawing before he could walk or talk. When he is not drawing monsters or spaceships piloted by monkeys, he loves to fight with his cat and walk his dog. He also enjoys meeting friends and reading comics. He lives near Madrid, Spain.

GERMAN TORRES has always loved to draw. He also likes to drive his van to the mountains and enjoy a little fresh air with his girlfriend and dogs. But what he really loves is traveling. He lives in a town near Barcelona, Spain, away from the noise of the city.